HOOKED ON HEAVEN

And Other Stories

HOOKED ON HEAVEN

And Other Stories

An Exclusive Short Story Collection
by Crossings Members

Crossings Book Club
Garden City, New York

Published by Crossings Book Club, 401 Franklin Avenue, Garden City, New York 11530.

Book design by Christos Peterson

ISBN: 1-58288-131-6

Printed in the United States of America

Contents

~∾

Introduction

Dear Reader,

This book has been a dream of ours ever since our first Crossings Voices fiction contest three years ago, when we first saw the many and various stories God had given to you, our members. What a joy it was to watch them unfold, and to be able to celebrate your talents with the rest of the membership. So it is with great pleasure that we offer here, for your entertainment and the encouragement of your faith, twelve stories that are true gems. From the love of a pet to a romantic encounter on a train, they represent just some of the ways God shows his care and concern for us. When you've got a few moments, or a nice rainy day, we can't think of a better book to have at your side.

For the record, six of the stories included here are Crossings Voices prize winners. From our first contest, we have:

> 1st prize: Pretty Pictures
> 2nd prize: Cañon de Alegría
> 3rd prize: Hooked on Heaven

From the second Crossings Voices contest, the following stories were winners:

1st prize: The Adoption
2nd prize: Just Down Whitmire Road
3rd prize: The Freedom Quilt

May you enjoy the efforts of these writers as much as we have.

In His Service,

Andrea Doering
Editor-in-Chief
New York, August 2004

HOOKED ON HEAVEN

And Other Stories

Hooked on Heaven

by Joan Janzen

I'M ABOUT TO tell you about the strangest day in the history of my hometown, Reeceville. It all began a couple of weeks ago when I was visiting Gramps and Gramma while my parents were out of town.

Gramps shifted gears on his green Ford pickup as we drove down the lane separating his farm from my folks' place. I was sitting right beside him watching wide-eyed as he did this using the hook attached to his right arm. Gramps had had his hook for as long as I knew him and long before that. He lost his arm in a threshing accident when he was nineteen years old, so he was more familiar with that hook than he was with his missing hand. In my whole lifetime of eight years, two months, and some days, I'd never seen anything as amazing as Gramps using that hook.

"What are you gonna do at town, Gramps?" I asked as

Gramps peered over my shoulder at the newly sprouting crops. It always scared me when he did that 'cause he wasn't paying attention to where he was driving. Just as the truck's tires crunched on the road's shoulder, Gramps directed his attention back to the road ahead.

"Gotta give the keys for the community hall to a fellow who's staying in town for a spell. The fellow says he's gonna conduct an evangelist meetin' at Reeceville tomorrow night."

"What's an evange-list meetin'?" I wanted to know, as I studied Gramps's face. I was quietly counting the number of lines and wrinkles to see if they would end up an even or an odd number, like I learned in math class.

"Well, Benny, an evangelist meeting is when someone goes around spreading religion, I suppose. I hardly see no cause for this feller to come to Reeceville. Folks already got their own religion. We've got a nice church and perd-near everyone attends real regular, but to each his own I guess," Gramps concluded. He slowed down the truck as he approached the lane to Emett Hobbs's place. "Emett asked if I'd give him a ride to town. He wants to pick up a few things at the store," Gramps explained.

"NO! Not Emett!" my thoughts screamed in silent protest. The truth was Emett Hobbs stunk. Clouds of body odor followed him wherever he went. I was none too pleased to have Emett and myself sharing the same small closed-in space.

We pulled up in front of Emett's old shack. I'm sure it hadn't seen a coat of paint in decades. Weather-worn flower boxes chock full of weeds hung sadly beneath mud-streaked windows. No one I'd ever talked to had actually ever been in

Emett's house. No matter how hard I tried to peer through the dirty windows, I could see absolutely nothing. The front door gaped open and Emett emerged wearing oily coveralls, a ripped green-plaid shirt, stained ball cap, and work boots that had seen better days. His black lab, Digger, followed closely at his heels.

"Hey Emett, ready to go?" Gramps yelled out the driver's window.

"Yup, sure am," Emett drawled, opening the truck door and sliding in next to me. I squished as close as I could to Gramps trying to avoid the smell, but it was no use. The sour scent crawled all over me. Gramps rolled down his window, which helped some.

"How you doin', Emett?" inquired Gramps. Asking Emett that particular question was a big mistake, 'cause Emett proceeded to tell Gramps exactly how he was doing. When Emett wasn't tellin' folks about his ailments and aches, he was complainin' about the crops, the weather, grain prices, or anything that popped into his head. As far as I knew, Gramps was the only friend Emett had. Everyone else about Reeceville left old smelly Emett alone. I allowed my mind to wander, drowning out Emett's voice as best I could.

Directly in front of us an old brown Buick crept along at a snail's pace. As Gramps pulled over to pass, I noted the driver's balding head glistening in the sun and long shoulder-length hair flapping in the wind, a rather gross combination to say the least. It was none other than Emil Stone. Folks called him Stoney. Stoney was as strange as Emett was smelly. Folks said Emil Stone had gone to Californy and had taken up with some woman. The story goes that she up and took off with a lot of his money. When Emil came home, folks started calling him Stoney because he had become as hard as stone.

He stayed pretty much to himself, except for attending social events or church services. Even then he'd sit by himself, arms crossed, wearing the same old brown suit.

Gramps shifted gears and the truck slowed down obediently as we approached Reeceville. The general store was at the edge of town. I could see a couple of the regulars sitting at the coffee table by the storefront window as we pulled to a stop. I kinda wondered what topic was brewin' with the coffee today.

Gramps opened his door and before he could get out of the truck I teased, "Hook me, Gramps!" Gramps wrapped his right arm and hook around me tightly, pulling me along with him out of the truck.

"I'm hooked on you big time, Benny. You're my boy!" Gramps chimed, as he had hundreds of times before. It was our private little joke. That meant only me and him thought it was funny.

The front door squeaked as Gramps opened it. The smells of tobacco and coffee filled my nostrils. Gramps handed me an orange pop from the vending machine. I sat beside Big Dan, the pig farmer, and wrapped my hot palms around the cold glass bottle. Ernett set about picking up the few grocery items he needed. Sitting next to me, Gramps leaned back in his chair and with his left hand removed a pouch of tobacco and cigarette wrappers from his shirt pocket. I was wishing my friends were here to see Gramps roll a cigarette with one hand. It was so cool!

Gramps balanced a cigarette paper on his knee and, clutching his tobacco pouch to his chest with his hook, he removed just the right amount of strawlike tobacco with his hand and dropped it onto the paper. Using his fingers he would roll that paper and tobacco into a tight tube, lick the edge of the paper, and seal it tight. Putting the cigarette between his lips he took a pack of matches from his pocket, and tucked them between his hook and his knee, igniting a match with his hand. He took the first puff and inhaled deeply, as I imitated the sucking motion. My mother would have given me a disapproving look if she'd have been there, but she wasn't.

"Hey, Ralph," Big Dan said to Gramps (Ralph was Gramps's other name), "see that poster over there?" Big Dan didn't pause for Gramps's reply. "Says some preacher's renting the town hall." My eyes followed Big Dan's fat finger to a poster that read HEAR ABOUT JESUS in bold letters.

"Yup, I'm going to give the fellow the keys soon as I leave here," Gramps responded.

"I think that preacher will be preachin' to himself. Ain't nobody gonna show up. We all does our duty and goes to church every Sunday and that's plain good enough," speculated Big Dan. I think he pretty much spoke for most of the folks in Reeceville, or at least that's the way I saw it. The other two men at the table nodded in silent agreement.

Gramps butted out the stub of his cigarette and nudged me to finish my pop quick-like. "Benny, time to go. I'll tell Emett to wait for us in the truck. The preacher fellow's staying next door at the old Hogan place. Reckon he's wanting those keys."

I followed Gramps through the squeaky door and over to the old green stucco house next door. As we waited for someone to answer our knock, I imagined the preacher to be old, balding, and overweight. My chin nearly dropped down to the sidewalk when a young man in his early twenties came to the door. He had warm, chocolate-brown eyes and a crop of freckles covered his nose and cheeks. Above all that was a mop of red curly hair.

"Good mornin' sir," he replied, his smile lighting up his entire face.

"Mornin'," Gramps responded. "You the fellow wanting to rent the town hall?"

"Sure am," he answered.

"Well, here's the keys," offered Gramps. Then, as an afterthought, he added, "This here's my grandson Benny and I'm Ralph Sinclair."

"Pleased to meet you," the young man responded as he held out his hand for a shake. "My name's Scott McMann."

Gramps scratched his head. "We used to have a feller we called Scotty McMann come around these parts. Haven't seen him for a couple of years now, though. He peddled house-wares and such. You any kin to him?" Gramps asked.

"That would be my grampa," informed Scott.

"Well, I'll be! You're Scotty McMann's grandson! He was quite a character. Sometimes he'd be wearin' a kilt when he came around. Was the darndest thing I've ever seen." Gramps laughed. "How's he doin' anyway?"

"Gramps passed away two months ago," Scott replied rather seriously.

"Sorry, son," Gramps shuffled his feet a bit awkwardly, suddenly breaking the silence with, "so you're a preacher, eh? Sure don't look the part."

"I've just got something I want to say," Scott replied.

"Preacher sounds pretty important. I'm just a regular guy."

I had kinda taken a shine to this young, handsome guy so I tugged at Gramps's sleeve. "Hey, Gramps. Can we invite him over for supper?"

"I, ah, gee, I guess, I suppose," Gramps stuttered, caught by surprise.

"Good," I piped up before Gramps could protest. "Gramma always cooks enough for ten people anyway."

"Well, I guess, if you're sure it's all right," Scott ventured. "I am kinda tired of eating macaroni and cheese."

That's how it came about that the preacher was sitting at Gramma's kitchen table smackin' his lips after a second helping of her apple pie. Have to admit Gramma was kind of cool toward Scott at first, always being a mite suspicious of preachers, but nothing warmed her heart more than someone willing to have a second piece of her apple pie.

"You have an appetite just like my grandson Seth. He could eat a horse and not gain an ounce," she laughed.

Gramps pushed away from the table. He never wasted any time dillydallying at the table after the meal was done. "Benny, why don't you show Scott around the farm?" he more ordered than asked.

I grabbed Scott's hand and pulled as he laughed, "Okay, okay, I'm coming!"

I showed him Gramps's prize pig, Homer the Hog, and the chickens, and even the ornery turkeys that would jump at you if you teased them.

"So are you and your grandparents coming to the meeting tomorrow night, Benny?" Scott asked.

"I don't rightly know. Gramma says we already got our

religion and we don't need another one." Pausing, I added, "And well, Gramps usually agrees with her, just to be safe."

"I'm not offering a religion; I'm offering Jesus." Scott corrected. "You've heard about Jesus at church, right?"

"Oh sure. He's a baby in a manger at Christmas," I spouted with pride. "He's all growed up and on a cross at Easter and after that he's standing around smiling wearing a bathrobe."

"You're absolute right, Benny," Scott laughed. "Jesus is alive and He needs a place to live. That's why you can ask Him to come into your heart and He will. All He asks is that you make your heart nice and clean before He comes in." I'd never heard anything like that before, but I told Scott I'd think about what he'd said. As for going to the meetin'—that would depend on Gramps and Gramma.

Next evening, Gramps pushed himself away from the supper table as usual. "Benny, how's about you and I check out this meetin' that young feller Scott's havin'?" he asked. I was game to go anywhere, even if it was just a religious meetin'.

Lookin' out the truck's windshield I could see none other than Emett standing at the end of his lane. Gramps slowed down as he drew near and rolled down his window. "What's up, Emett?" he asked.

"Digger's been wheezin' peculiar-like," whined Emett. "Can I hitch a ride to town to see Vet Dirks?"

"We'll be in town a while at that young fellow's meetin', but you're welcome to come if you don't mind waitin' at the hall till it's over," Gramps offered.

So, off we went—Gramps, Emett, and me. I was beginning to wonder if anything else could possibly be worse than riding in a truck with Emett two days in a row, when just yonder up ahead sat the answer to my silent question. Stoney's old Buick was parked at the side of the road, hood open, flashers on. Gramps slowed down once again and pulled over beside the Buick.

"Car trouble?" he inquired as Stoney's head emerged from under the hood.

"Yup," he growled. "Stupid thing done quit on me. Don't want to be late for that meetin'."

Yes, there was something worse than riding in a truck with Emett two days in a row. It was riding in a truck with Gramps, Emett, and Stoney. Stoney sat stone-faced, eyes staring straight ahead, arms crossed in front of his chest while Emett continued complaining about whatever he could think of. I pinched my nose with my left hand and stuck my right index finger in my right ear.

Vehicles were rolling into the community hall parking lot in a steady stream. Evidently word had got around the young man was old Scotty McMann's grandson and everyone was curious as all . . . well, they was curious to see what this meetin' was all about. Scott was standing at the front door greeting people as they arrived. Gramps and I shook his hand, but old Stoney walked right on by and seated himself at the very back of the hall. Emett had gone off to see the vet and said he'd be back shortly.

When all the folks had kinda settled down in their seats, Scott went up to the front and sat on a stool strumming his guitar. He began to sing a song about the blood of Jesus and never seemed to pay no mind to all us folks sitting in front of him. He just sang like he was all by himself somewheres. I can't rightly explain it.

Soon as he'd finished the song, he propped his guitar against the stool and looked out at us all. "A lot of you folks are here tonight 'cause you heard Scotty McMann was my grampa. I'm right glad you came," Scott began while taking a battered black book out of his shirt pocket. "This here book belonged to my grampa. It's not a Bible, just a book full of people's names. People from Reeceville who he would visit on his rounds selling his wares. Got names here like Beckett, Hobbs, Sinclair, Stone, Follie . . . and lots more. Before Grampa died, he gave me this book. He told me he'd been prayin' for everyone listed here for more than fifteen years." Scott stopped to wipe his eyes. "I didn't know what to do with this book, but as the days went by I knew I had to come to Reeceville and tell you about Grampa. I want to tell you what he would have told you if he was here. He'd say 'Sonny, there's no friend like Jesus. He loves you more than any friend ever could.' I'm not gonna preach today, but if you want Jesus to be your friend, come up front and I'll be glad to pray with you."

Having finished his talk, Scott picked up his guitar and began to strum and sing softly. Everyone was so-o-o quiet I could hear the crickets chirping. Sunbeams shone through the side doors that were open to let in the cool breeze. I saw someone's shadow fall on the floor by the door. The silhouette looked a lot like Emett. I guessed he had been listening by the door.

We'd been sitting quite a spell listening to the guitar and Scott's voice when I heard scurrying feet shuffling on the floor. I turned my head to see Old Lady Potts in such a hurry to get to the front she forgot to use her cane. Instead she held it horizontally with the hook sticking out behind her. Funny thing was, Stoney was right behind her, cussing and swearin' and pullin on her cane, but Old Lady Potts just kept on truckin' forward. That's when I noticed the hook of her cane was caught on old Stoney's belt loop. She pulled that poor old boy straight to the front where he stood making this strange blubberin' sound. I feared he might be fixin' to have a heart attack or something, but then I realized old Stoney was cryin' like a baby.

That's not all. Emett came out of his hiding spot, head hanging low, and strolled over beside Stoney. I didn't think nothing could surprise me much more than that, when Gramps reached over and put his arm around me. "How about it, Benny? Wanna go up front with me?" he asked. Truth was I'd been so busy watchin' everyone else I hadn't really taken much thought about myself. I figured anything good enough for Gramps was good enough for me.

After the meeting was over, the four of us piled in the truck. Old Stoney had a smile stretched from one ear clear over to the other. Surprisingly, Emett never said more than two words all the way home, while Stoney babbled on and on and on.

"I think Jesus hooked Emett and old Stoney real good," I whispered to Gramps.

"You know, son, I think Jesus hooked us all," he whispered right back at me.

The next day almost everyone in the Reeceville area gathered for Sunday church service. Stoney was there wearing a silly smile. Emett looked proud enough to bust his buttons wearin' Gramps's suit. He even smelled good. Old Lady Potts looked somewhat younger than I remembered. Scott stood at the back of the building happily observing. Even though it all seemed rather strange, I got a hankerin' that things is gonna get stranger yet.

Pretty Pictures

by Jean Flora Glick

～

SHE DOES HEAVY-duty work," said my friend Marge Webster, recommending her cleaning woman, Florence. "Tackles the tough stuff like windows, shower stalls, and even ovens! But remember, Linda, she's no spring chicken."

Despite the warning, I was surprised that first morning when Florence creaked up our deck steps. She struggled in our back door, huffing as though she'd stair-climbed the Empire State Building. Her reddish-gray hair looked like she'd stuck her finger in an electrical outlet and hot-wired her head.

As she mopped our kitchen, Florence groaned when she stooped and her arthritic knees protested in a Rice Krispies chorus of snap, crackle, and pop. After she left, my practical, efficient husband of thirty-three years complained, "Your cleaning woman doesn't attend to details. She swept the garage but hung the shop broom on the wrong peg!"

"Florence does the best she can," I said, "and she charges next to nothing."

"She does? Okay, you can keep her," Bob replied. He loves cheap. I've even teased him, saying he should sign payroll checks for his accounting business with his nickname, "Bottom-line Bob."

Whenever Florence cleaned, Bob grumbled and nit-picked. I defended her because I felt sorry for her. Yet, having Florence was inconvenient. She didn't have a phone, didn't drive. Early Saturdays, I'd pick her up, do my errands, and hurry back to take her home. Just seeing the house where she stayed depressed me. It was a ramshackle place with a saggy front porch. I knew Florence worked as a live-in caregiver for alcoholic old Mr. Middleton.

One Saturday I heard Florence on her hands and knees scouring our shower. Like a novice bagpiper, she wheezed with each swipe of the scrub brush. Despite her efforts, Bob said, "I see Florence put new toilet paper in the holder. You know I like the toilet tissue on the spindle with the paper hanging over the top of the roll. Not coming out from under it. Would you please tell her?"

I promised I'd remind her.

"Doesn't she live on Depot Street?" he inquired. "That's the worst part of town. Can we trust her? Wouldn't want any of my coin collection to disappear."

I assured him Florence was honest, but I checked by leaving cash on my bedroom vanity. There was $65.47 before she cleaned and $65.47 after she left.

Once, in early August, I fixed lunch for Florence and me.

As I bit hungrily into my ham-salad sandwich, I glanced up, and there Florence sat, her frowsy head bent, her gnarled hands clasped in prayer as she whispered, "Come Lord Jesus / Our guest to be / Bless this food / Bestowed by Thee." Quickly, I bowed my head and mumbled grace, too. In truth, Florence's quiet reverence and humble faith touched me.

Later, as she vacuumed the family room, I brought her iced tea. Plopping in Bob's lounge chair, she sighed, "Thank you. A cold drink sure hits the spot."

Pointing to our family portrait, she commented, "What a nice lookin' son you have. A child can be such a blessing."

"Yes, Todd is. He starts college soon, and I don't know how I'll let my 'baby' go. Do you have children?"

"I'm all alone in the world, ma'am. Many years ago I was married to a good man, but I've had some grief. We had a son, and then our second child, a little girl, was born with a problem. Bad blood, that's what the nurses called it. They told us the baby needed all new blood, that her blood and mine didn't match. After a few hours, she died. Though I've heard that nowadays they can fix a baby with bad blood. But not then."

"Where's your son now?"

"Well, ma'am, my husband Joe and I lived in a rental close to the sawmill, just south of the railroad tracks. Nothin' fancy, but I always kept a clean house. Little Joey was our pride and joy. First thing Big Joe walked in from workin' at the sawmill, he'd lift Joey to his knee and bounce him, 'Giddy-up, giddy-up, horsey man . . . Ride him, ride him, fast as you can.' Joey would giggle. Thought his daddy was the funniest man.

"After work, when Joey heard Big Joe whistlin' up the front walk, he'd race to the screen door, waving his little arms, poundin' on the screen sayin' 'Da-da, Da-da.' I'd have a good meal ready. We were real happy, the three of us."

I sipped my tea, the ice cubes clinking.

"So this August afternoon," Florence continued, "I'm sittin' and rockin' on the porch swing waitin' for Big Joe and Joey. They'd gone to the grocery to get Joe a pack of cigarettes, and I'm rockin' and rockin'. Letting the air cool my face. Maybe I should stir up a glass of iced tea for Joe, I thought, and I'd decided to do that very thing when I heard it.

"It was awful loud, that sound. There was the whooo-whooo of the 4:45 New York Central rumblin' by, then this terrible bang. Scrunchin' metal. Glass breakin'. Brakes squealin'. Folks had complained to the railroad about how dangerous the crossing was. But the railroad people said there wasn't enough traffic to put up a flasher or a wooden arm."

"Oh, Florence!" I gasped.

"That awful boom fairly shook the porch. My heart slid down to my toes. Not Big Joe. Not Joey, I screamed in my head. But it was. It surely was."

A lump formed in my throat as Florence said, "So I've looked out for myself since then. These days, I only work for my favorites, like you. My steam's almost gone."

"What brought you to Collinsville?" I asked.

"My cousin told me Mr. Middleton needed someone to cook and clean. He doesn't have any legs, lost them both to sugar diabetes. He's got a temper and throws things when he drinks too much, but I thank the Lord for a roof over my head."

"He sounds mean!"

"I'm used to his shenanigans. It's tolerable, that is, until

Mr. Middleton's grown kids come to mooch. They beg me to cook for them, and I do. But they never say, 'Thank you, Florence. Nice meal, Florence.'

"Instead after they've eaten off of us until Mr. Middleton's food stamps are gone, they leave. First of the month, Social Security time, here they come. After every visit, I find stuff missin'. Once, they unscrewed the lightbulbs from the ceiling fixture and took them. Imagine that!"

"They're taking advantage of you, Florence. You should move out!"

"No place else to go. And the old man needs me. I don't own nothin' fine, but I know the Lord loves me 'cause of that Bible verse, 'Blessed are the poor in heart, for they will see God.'"

Amused, I gently corrected her. "You must mean the Beatitudes. The one in Matthew 5:8. Except it says 'Blessed are the *pure* in heart, for they will see God.'"

"Don't that beat all!" Florence chuckled. "Blessed are the pure in heart . . . that's a good one on me, Mrs. Spencer."

Shaking her head, she repeated, "Blessed are the pure in heart."

"What version of the Bible do you have?" I inquired.

"Oh, I don't have a Bible. I remembered the verse from Preacher Brown's sermon."

While she worked, I rummaged through our bookshelves. I found a Bible, one with brightly colored pictures that Todd favored as a child.

"Florence, take this Bible. And here, take some extra lightbulbs, too."

As I drove her home, she thanked me repeatedly. She held

the Bible in her crippled hands as gently as a mother cradles a newborn.

That evening, Bob lifted the coffee canister, spied a sticky brown ring on the counter, and sputtered, "Florence didn't move this when she cleaned. Get rid of her."

When I quickly recapped Florence's life story, he and I came to a compromise. I'd have her once a month; we'd hire his cleaning service, the one that did his office, other times.

Before our Thanksgiving dinner party, I was overwhelmed with preparations and Bob suggested I hire Florence to help me. After she cleaned, I noticed she'd missed cobwebs criss-crossing the chandelier. She apologized, "Sorry, ma'am. Must need new glasses."

I figured that was a hint, considering her upcoming birth-day. In fact, I'd have sent her money for new glasses, but Todd's college tuition came due. Instead, I mailed a birthday card with a ten-dollar bill inside.

By now, bitter cold had blitzed Indiana. Indeed, it was an ice storm that finally sealed Florence's fate. When our elec-tricity went off, Bob climbed a step stool to reset our kitchen clock above the refrigerator. He found enough dust to write his name. I had to agree with him; Florence was slipping.

Reluctantly, I told Florence I'd not need her again until spring. She looked surprised, then nodded her head, as if she understood. I sent her a Christmas card and a five-dollar bill, and gave her name and address to a church group that deliv-ered food baskets to the needy.

In January, Marge called, telling me Florence was in the hospital. Pneumonia.

Driving home from work, I passed the hospital, intending

to stop. No, I'd better wait. I'd worked overtime . . . So I sent Florence a friendly note inside a get-well card.

But I waited too long. January twenty-ninth I read Florence's obituary in the newspaper—age sixty-seven, no survivors except distant cousins. Preceded in death by a husband and two children. Calling hours at Parker's Funeral Parlor were the next evening, when I was hostess for Ladies Circle at the church. I mailed a sympathy card to Mr. Middleton, and Bob agreed we should send flowers. I'd have attended Florence's funeral if I hadn't been so swamped at work.

That evening, Marge phoned. "Mr. Middleton sent his son over and asked me to call you. When Florence left for the hospital, she told him that should anything happen to her, she had something for you. Stop by his house, will you?"

I dreaded going, but I was curious. What could Florence have left for me? I drove to Depot Street and knocked on Mr. Middleton's door. A wizened old man in a wheelchair opened the door. Tobacco juice dribbled down his chin, and his eyes bored through me like a hot poker. When I explained who I was, he motioned me inside. He wheeled into a tiny room where I glimpsed a cot, chair, and table. Reaching under a pillow on the cot, he pulled out a Bible.

"Florence said you loaned her this," he said. "She was real careful with it. Said she wanted it returned to you."

"Oh, no, she misunderstood," I gasped. "I gave the Bible to her. I wanted her to have her own Bible to read."

Mr. Middleton shook his head. "She couldn't read. Turned the pages every night, though. Said it had real pretty pictures."

A paper, crisply folded, fell from the Bible. I picked it up, recognizing the note that I'd enclosed with her get-well card. I'd written, "You are a woman of strong faith and you're definitely 'pure' in heart. See you this spring."

"Did you read her mail to her, Mr. Middleton?"

"Nope. Never did. She was real private with her personal stuff."

Tears in my eyes, I backed out the door. Half choked, I mumbled, "I'll miss her. She was such a special person. I'll really miss her."

Mr. Middleton replied, "She thought the world of you, too, Mrs. Spencer. Why, she said many a time how proud she was to work for such a good Christian woman."

I stumbled down the steps fully realizing who really was the good Christian woman. And regretfully, I could never tell Florence that.

A week later, I shelved a new book and saw Florence's picture Bible. Flipping through the pages, I tried to see them through her eyes. I picked up the phone, traced my finger down the directory, located the number, and dialed. This call was in honor of Florence.

A pleasant female voice greeted me. "Hello. How may I help you? You've reached Volunteer Tutors for Literacy."

Just Down Whitmire Road

by Karen Milasincic

JANIE MUST HAVE been up and down that lonely road on her bike at least thirty times. It had been Susan's bike, then Vickie's, now hers, and would soon be Jeff's. Thirty round trips and still no sign of anyone anywhere near thirteen years old. Not even anyone Jeff's age. It wouldn't matter to him; he was like Daddy's puppy. They'd moved into the ancient farmhouse Saturday morning, and everything Janie owned was unpacked by noon. It was after seven Sunday night and Janie Birch was in search of a friend, or she'd face riding the bus to a strange school alone. Why did she have to start now with only five weeks left until summer vacation?

Janie, who had never been the new girl until now, had lived all her life in Bethlehem, Pennsylvania. Friends were plentiful. Luther Birch's meager livelihood dissolved with the layoffs at Bethlehem Steel, and he moved his family, except for Vickie, who'd started a family of her own, to Saxonburg: pop. 1529. They were about an hour from Pittsburgh, where he'd found work, but here real estate was more affordable than in the suburbs. This far from the city he could get a nice piece of land for his money, and he intended to farm it some. "A way to make ends meet," he explained to Joyce and the kids. The ends never met in Bethlehem, where Daddy had eighteen years in at the mill, and Janie doubted they'd meet here, either. Mom didn't worry. She'd always put her faith in both Luther Birch and God.

The two-mile stretch of Whitmire Road had only eleven other houses. Blooming dogwoods brightened the patches of woods in between. Janie turned back for the place she'd be calling home, where she knew Mom would have some encouraging words for her. Just one more incline up ahead before the Birch farm. She needed to build a good speed from the downhill, or her tired legs wouldn't take her around again.

She whizzed by it every other time, and never noticed that pothole. Janie landed alongside the road with gravel embedded in her bloody palm. Tears pooled in her green eyes, more for the sadness building inside than the sting in her hand. She felt alone in this new place. Mom, Daddy, and Jeff were excited about learning how to farm. Nineteen-year-old Susan hoped to get an apartment as soon as she got hired by one of the local salons. Janie was on her own.

"I'm comin'! Don't you move!" Janie was so startled by the old lady's voice that she didn't hear the admonition and jumped to her feet. It was the woman who waved from her porch rocker every time Janie had passed. Her face was worn, more so than Janie's Grandma Bateman, but her eyes were bright and her smile so kind that Janie followed her into a run-down house she'd have otherwise taken for abandoned. Inside, the furnishings were few. A mason jar of lilacs scented the kitchen. Janie's eyes beamed into the next room where a lovely walnut upright piano stood. Stacked neatly on top was a life story of music.

"My name is Annie Whitmire. You can call me Annie." She placed a steaming cup of tea by Janie's washed and bandaged hand. "Soon as your hand heals up, you come try it out— the piano. That's what you're ogling, isn't it? Not much else to ogle in here."

"Well, I don't know how to play, but it sure is pretty."

"I can't play anymore, either. Look at these hands." Annie's knuckles were gnarled, and her fingers seemed to bend in all directions. "But I can take what I have up here," she pointed toward her snowy white waves, "and put it in these," and she took gentle hold of Janie's fingers.

"Daddy says we can't afford piano lessons just now."

"I don't charge for piano lessons anymore. I have all the money I need." Annie's laugh echoed within the near-bare kitchen. "You come back. It's been near seven years since my hands quit on me—1971—the summer after my husband died. I'll get Fred Geibel out here to tune her up." Annie sounded almost as thrilled as Janie was by the proposition. "That piano needs playin'!"

Five weeks wasn't much time to penetrate a closed circle of eighth-graders who'd known each other all their lives. Some were polite. Some weren't. Janie didn't find any friends at the Saxonburg Junior High School that year, but afternoons she found one just down Whitmire Road.

"Whitmires up and down this road when I married Walter," Annie told Janie after their daily lesson. "They've gotten married, moved on, even passed on." Janie kept playing when the lesson was over since she had nothing on which to practice her assignments at home. Annie moved from her teacher's position on the bench over to her rocker. "I'm the last Whitmire around here. My Raymond, he's the only child I could have, he doesn't come 'round no more. See him about once a year." Janie stared into the black-and-white photo hanging alone on the wall by the piano. A uniformed young man looked back with no expression.

"Where's he live, Annie?"

"Pittsburgh. He used to play." She nodded toward the piano. "Beautifully too. Fell in love with the bottle somewhere along the line and don't make time for nothing else. Broke his Daddy's heart. Neither one of us ever drank a drop. He still shows up at Christmas, drunk usually, more often if he needs some money. How can a mother turn away her only child?" Annie's eyes filled up, and she shook her head. "Play, play," Annie said, and waved for Janie to continue. Janie moved through her exercises without err, thriving on the delight she'd restored to Annie's face. She was already halfway through her first book.

Janie wouldn't miss an afternoon of Annie's encouragement and wisdom, and she didn't leave without doing some small chore. The yard got mowed and raked. The porch rail and front door got painted. Flowerbeds got weeded. Windows got washed. Janie carried screens home, one by one, to be mended by Daddy. Raymond showed up one late July evening snorting over how much of her savings his mother was throwing away on all the unnecessary primping.

Farming caught on with the rest of the Birches, especially eager young Jeff. But at least once a week Joyce Birch stole away for a chance to hear her Janie play. She asked for "Amazing Grace" every time and made a mother's production about the week's progress. One Friday afternoon when the tiger lilies stretched up high around Annie's porch, the three of them swayed on the porch swing, shiny and white as new, and finished a jar of iced tea. "You mays-well not be surprised at Janie's talent, Joyce. I've not seen many naturals in all my teaching years, but she's one of 'em. She's found her passion. You can see it. She's through with a book most kids spend a year on."

"I'm certainly thankful she has you, Annie, and a place to play. She started asking about lessons first time she ever saw a piano at her friend's house in Bethlehem."

"I'm just glad to hear my piano again, Joyce." There was a pause when only the screeching crows were heard. Annie began speaking again with a thought that had been simmering in her mind. "I know it's a way off, but there's some good schooling down in the city for music. Might be something to think about ahead of time. I had one student who's off writing some of her own music now and getting paid for it! Sharon had that love for it same as Janie."

Janie sat quiet while the two women discussed her future. College wasn't anything the Birches ever talked about. Vickie got married the summer after high school. Susan waitressed her way through beauty school. Mark had eight more years to think about it. Janie turned fourteen on the fifth of July, but after only three months of playing she knew she wanted music to be part of her life.

"Things are sort of tight at our house, Annie. But there are scholarships for those kinds of things. And God'll work things out, I know. He brought Janie to you, didn't he?"

"He did. And He will."

Afternoons still hit ninety degrees, but it was back to school in three days. Janie wasn't concerned about shopping for school clothes this year. How much could she get for fifty dollars anyway? She was only concerned about the hours school would take away from her visits with Annie. She planned on asking if she could just have the bus drop her off at Annie's each afternoon.

The bus got her to Annie's long dirt driveway Monday through Friday by three o'clock. She stayed till 4:45 and walked home to set the table for supper, always ready at five. Janie lingered one Friday to browse through the stacks of music on top of Annie's old Baldwin. "Is there any more music in here?" she asked, reaching for the piano bench.

"Oh, no, no, no." Annie did a quick shuffle from the kitchen. "I don't keep any music in there." She pressed on the bench lid. "You look in this stack further to the right," she said. "I keep it in order of difficulty, left to right. There's enough on top here to keep you busy through winter, I'd say. More over in the closet when it's time."

Janie began playing from the music in Annie's closet nearly two years after her first lesson. She'd picked up two good friends her freshman year of high school, but still spent more time with Annie than anyone else except Mom. It was their combined effort that convinced Janie to compete in the school talent show near the end of tenth grade. She came in second place to a senior soprano who gave an impressive rendition of Olivia Newton-John's "I Honestly Love You." Annie rode along in the family's Plymouth station wagon to the show, and Daddy treated everyone to a vanilla custard at Goob's Dairy Bar on the way home. The financial situation had stabilized by the family's second year in Saxonburg, but college was still a shaky topic. "The community college maybe, but no fancy university in Pittsburgh," Daddy had said.

Janie went on keeping up Annie's yard and took over the heavy cleaning too. The arthritis rendered Annie's hands nearly useless. Janie cut up vegetables from Daddy's garden for soup and went to the A & P with Mom to bring dry goods in for Annie's cupboards every other week. Not once did she see Raymond Whitmire around again. He never showed up to shovel snow in the winter or cut a blade of grass in the summer. Janie didn't mind. She had a seventy-four-year-old best friend.

It was halfway through her senior year, and Janie was coming to the bottom of the music in Annie's closet. Her friends were applying to Pitt and Penn State. She begged Daddy so much that he at least let her apply to Duquesne. She'd kept up her grades, and there were scholarships to hope for.

Janie splashed her way down the slushy road the first Sunday in January, eager to work on a new piece of sheet music Vickie sent for Christmas. Puffy wet flakes drenched her hair, and her sneakers were soaked through by the time she stepped inside Annie's warm kitchen. The copper teakettle whistled, and the room was filled with steam.

"Annie, your water's done." Janie moved the kettle off the gas burner. "Annie, it's boiled near dry. Annie?" She poured the little bit of water into the cup waiting with tea bag, sugar cube, and sprinkling of milk inside, and carried it into the piano room.

Annie was waiting for Janie in her padded rocker as usual, her yellow and blue afghan draped over her lap, dozing. "Annie, I have your tea ready." Janie touched Annie's crippled hand to wake her. It was cool. Her eyes were slightly open, but there was no life in them. Janie let the steaming cup crash to the hardwood floor. "Annie! Wake up! Annie!" she cried. Then she dropped to the floor at Annie's feet where she stayed sobbing for at least the first half hour of her life without Annie. Finally she stood and went for the new piece of music. Through tear-blurred eyes she played "Softly and Tenderly" as if Annie sat listening like hundreds of times before. It was a courageous attempt with pitiful results. She needed to go for help, but she felt for the first time since that long-ago day an uncontrollable urge to see what was inside the piano bench. She lifted the lid slowly. A gasp, then confusion quickly followed to settle in with her grief. As if she might have an explanation, Janie looked to her friend, then back inside the bench. There were rows of dollar bills, rubber-banded in stacks, packed tightly within. Janie's trembling fingers counted fifty dollars in one of the stacks, which were four deep. There looked to be a hundred or more of them. A manila folder rested off to the side in the bed of cash. She flipped it open, and found Annie's will and a hand-written note. The words were barely legible. Each shaky letter reflected the pain in its forming.

Janie,

I have saved every dollar I made from giving piano lessons to further the gift of music. You have been much more than my student. You have been my friend. Use this money to help you get to Duquesne and of course the piano is yours too.

God Bless You,
Your loving friend,
Annie Whitmire

Reverend Eugene Henderson escorted Raymond Whitmire out of Fox Funeral Home when he made a terrible scene with the Birches. He accused them of soaking up all his inheritance from his "senile" mother. Since Raymond could never keep a wife long enough to have children, there were no other family members to pay respects. No biological family at least. But lining the hallways were dozens of families from all around Saxonburg who had been blessed by Annie's teaching, and one family had even flown in from Nashville. At the funeral Janie fought with every nerve to move her fingers through all the notes of both "Softly and Tenderly" and "Amazing Grace" on Saxonburg Presbyterian Church's grand piano.

There would be more shaky nerves, bigger audiences, and grander pianos for Janie one day. Thanks to a best friend she found on Whitmire Road in Saxonburg, Janie was the first of the Birches to have hopes of college. And she had "the gift." Just like Mom said, "God'll work it out."

The Adoption

by Virginia Roark

~~~~

When she heard the roar of a car engine from down the road, Ruth opened the screen door to catch sight of the vehicle as it crested the hill. It was a pickup truck, with an unfamiliar driver at the wheel. He waved cordially as he passed. Ruth waved back, and then sat down on the porch steps.

Her heart was pounding after that false alarm. She looked at the sun streaming through the branches of the pine tree in the front yard, trying to focus. She and Tracie climbed that tree to the top when they were nine, thrilled by their accomplishment only to be punished when they descended for getting pitch all over their good clothes. It was such a good tree to climb, with its branches evenly spaced like so many stair steps. Every kid who lived here or visited climbed it. Including the foster children who occasionally came with Tracie. And coming this time was just another foster kid, Ruth told herself.

Tracie was her best friend from grade school through high school. The girl who used to pick up every stray animal that crossed her path now picked up stray kids. Tracie had been keeping foster children since her own children had grown up and moved out. She sometimes brought them to the farm for a visit, wide-eyed little kids and insolent teens, all showing in their individual way that they were hurting. This time Tracie was hurting, too, and needed her help. Tracie's mother, who lived by herself, had fallen and broken her back. Tracie had called Ruth from the hospital.

"This is the end of independent living," she said to Ruth. "I'm going to bring her home with me. But I'll have to stop the foster care. It's actually a good time, because I only have Stacia . . . that's what I'm calling about. Could you take Stacia for a few weeks?"

"Can't they find someone else? I mean, a more permanent home? It's not good to shuttle kids around every few weeks."

"It takes a little while. I called Social Services to get an emergency placement when I went to the hospital with my mother, and they took her to the Millers! If my mother hadn't been in intensive care, I would have come home immediately just to keep Stacia out of there."

"The Millers? Isn't that the place—"

"Where the father is suspected of molesting two little girls. Yes. Oh, I just can't let Stacia stay in a place like that. The kid has been through so much already . . . Ruth, do you think you could keep her until I get my mother home? Would it be all right with Jess?"

"My Jess? You know he wouldn't mind. Besides, he's at a convention until next week." But this was Stacia. Ruth sighed.

She felt trapped into saying yes. "I can't say no this time, Traci. Jess Junior has a summer job pitching hay for his cousin, and the twins are at camp until August."

"Ruth, you are a lifesaver. I mean for Stacia, not for me. Mom will be moved into a regular room tomorrow, and then I can dare leave her long enough to pick up Stacia and drive out to the farm."

So Tracie was coming to Ruth with the eight-year-old girl who had been in foster care since she was two. That's all Ruth knew about her, except for the one other thing. As she saw Tracie's beat-up minivan finally pull into the driveway, she felt a wave of panic. *Please, God, don't let them see my fear.*

"We made it!" The same old Tracie burst out of the driver's seat looking only a little harried for her recent stresses. She gave Ruth a hug, then turned toward her passenger, who was emerging from the other side. Ruth saw a slender, blond-headed girl, tall for her age. Her straight hair fell gently around her shoulders like corn silk. Tracie went over to her, and the girl smiled at her foster mother. Ruth was stunned at what she saw. The girl was remarkably beautiful. Her large almond-shaped eyes were deep gray-blue, framed by milky skin. Her lips were full, and her smile revealed straight white teeth.

"Hello, Stacia. I'm Ruth. Come in, both of you, and have something to drink. Tracie, can you stay for a cup of coffee?"

"I'll take you up on that, because I've got three more hours of driving left."

Ruth poured some coffee for Tracie, and got some milk and cookies for Stacia. Stacia sat down obediently, then looked up and asked, "Please, may I go to the bathroom?"

"Oh, of course, honey. Let me show you where it is. And

then after this you just go when you need to. You don't have to ask." She guided the girl down the hall, and then went back to join Tracie.

"Tracie, she's beautiful. It's too bad she couldn't be adopted."

"Yes, it's too bad." Tracie didn't say anything more. She wasn't going to make this easy. Ruth was going to have to ask.

"Does she—has she been tested?"

"Yes. And no, she isn't HIV positive."

Ruth breathed a sigh of relief. "That's good news. She's adoptable, then."

Tracie snorted. "She's adoptable in any case, if the right parents came along. But when they find out her mother was a junkie and a prostitute, nobody's interested. If they know her mother had AIDS, there's nothing you can say to them to prove Stacia is healthy. And it's such a shame. Stacia is not only pretty, she's very bright. It's amazing how well-adjusted she is for the life she's had to live."

The women's discussion ended as Stacia walked back into the kitchen, sat down, and drank her milk complacently. It was almost as if she were acting a role: just tell her what to do and she'd do it.

"I really have to get going." Tracie rose and walked around to Stacia. She gave the little girl a big hug. "Stacia, I'll call you after I get settled over there. And I'll be back in a few weeks. Have fun. I think you'll like the farm."

Stacia smiled. She watched Tracie go without showing any of the signs of anxiety most kids would under similar circumstances. Did Stacia ever let her guard down? What was she really feeling?

"Stacia, I think you'll like the farm, too," Ruth said. "What would you like to do?"

"I like to read, and I watch television," Stacia answered readily.

Ruth thought for a moment. "Do you like animals? We have cows, and pigs, and sheep, and dogs—"

"Do you have any cats?"

"Well, yes. They live in the barn. They're not pets, the same way some cats are. They catch the mice and rats in the barn. Would you like to see them?"

Stacia nodded, with eagerness on her face.

As they walked to the barn, Ruth automatically went through her "Barn Cat" lecture. "These cats have a job, to keep the mice from eating the grain. So we don't keep them in the house, or feed them a lot of cat food. Sometimes people ask us if we have any kittens, and we often do have some we can give away." She stopped short, remembering there was no mother or father with Stacia to whom she could turn and beg, "Could we get one, *please*?" But Stacia hadn't seemed to take in Ruth's last words. Her eyes scanned the barnyard, searching for the first sign of feline activity.

"There it is!" she cried suddenly.

"It" was Tiger, the yellow tom who was the self-appointed door guard. He sauntered up to them, rubbing on Stacia's legs.

"May I pick it up?" Normally, Ruth would have said no, continuing her lecture about how the cat might become frightened and scratch her. But Tiger wouldn't hurt anyone, and this might be Stacia's only chance to pet a cat.

Before Ruth could speak, though, Stacia gave herself an answer.

"No, I'm a stranger, and I shouldn't touch it." Learned from some "Never-Talk-to-Strangers" school program, no doubt. Stacia stood grinning as Tiger brushed about her legs and purred. When he tired of this activity, he went back into the barn, and Stacia and Ruth followed.

"I want to show you Oreo's kittens, if we can find them," Ruth said. "They're real little—they haven't opened their eyes yet." She found them in the straw-lined crate she'd provided for Oreo. That was lucky; mother cats often took their kittens to a place where it was hard for humans to locate them. "Here they are! Oreo has five kittens. Three are tiger-striped, like her, one's white, and the other's black. But where's the black one?" She felt around the box gingerly.

"Ruth . . ."

Ruth looked up, and Stacia pointed to a round dark ball next to the wall.

"Why, it's the kitten!" Ruth exclaimed. "How did it get there?" She picked it up and put it back in the crate. Oreo, already ruffled by the intrusion, got up and circled the crate, lying with her back to them. Her other four kittens nestled themselves inside their mother's arch, and found a nipple. But the black kitten huddled in the corner of the box, turning away from its mother.

"Here's your lost baby," Ruth said, placing the black kitten next to the others. The mother immediately rotated again, nudging the other kittens back between her legs and ignoring the black one. The mother had rejected the kitten. "Nature's Law," Jess called it. Mother cats sometimes rejected the runt or a kitten with something wrong with it. It would be dead by tomorrow. Oh, why did Stacia have to see this?

Stacia stared into the box. "Why isn't the mother feeding the black kitten?"

Ruth thought fast. "It may be too tired to eat right now."

"Will it starve?" Stacia was thinking faster than Ruth. She startled Ruth by asking, "Can *we* feed it?"

"Oh, honey, it's so hard to feed a kitten by hand." Ruth had let her boys try this a few times, just to show them it wasn't her hard-heartedness that caused the kittens to die.

"Please?" Stacia turned her face up to Ruth's, her large eyes dark with emotion. Ruth melted from the unexpected passion.

"Well, we can try. But it's not easy." She got a clean rag and wrapped the kitten in it to carry it to the house. In the kitchen, she found an eyedropper and mixed up some watered-down formula they used for the lambs. "Now sit down, and hold the dropper next to his mouth. Squeeze a little so the milk comes out by drops. But don't try to push it into his mouth. He has to suck it himself."

Stacia picked up on Ruth's reference to the kitten as "he." "We don't know yet if it's a girl or boy," she said. "I went to this girl's house once, and they had kittens. They couldn't tell 'til they were older. So we'd better give it a name that could be for a girl or boy. They called their black cat Molasses. I think that could be a girl or a boy, couldn't it?"

Ruth smiled and nodded, getting the sinking feeling she'd made a terrible mistake. She philosophized that at least she could give the child a few more hours of happiness. She showed her how to rub Molasses's tummy with a wet wash-cloth, the way a mother cat stimulated the bowels.

"Instead of diapers," Ruth explained. "But the mother cat eats it. We won't do that."

"Ugh!" Stacia grimaced, and then she and Ruth laughed.

Stacia sat all afternoon with the kitten in her lap. Every few minutes she would call out, "It's eating!" and then, "No, I guess not." She came to the table for dinner only after Ruth offered to hold the kitten while the little girl ate. After dinner, they watched television while Stacia sat on the floor with the kitten still in her lap. Finally Ruth said, "I need to show you your room, Stacia. You should be going to bed."

"But the kitten! Can it sleep with me?"

"You might roll over on it. I'll keep trying to feed it until I go to bed."

Stacia stared into space then tried again. "I can stay right here and hold it all night. Is that okay?"

Ruth sighed. She had been hoping to separate her from the kitten so that it wouldn't die in her arms. "All right. Just this once. I'll get you a blanket and pillow."

When Ruth finally went to bed herself, Stacia was wrapped up in a blanket on the living-room floor. She was propped to a half-sitting position by two pillows so that she could continue to hold the eyedropper near the kitten's mouth. Ruth lay wide awake in her bed for several hours, staring into the darkness and thinking about abandoned kids and kittens.

Ruth woke early and hurried down to the living room. Stacia was asleep, but still propped up with the kitten beside her. Milk had oozed out on the blanket as well as the rag the kitten was wrapped up in. As Ruth came closer, she could smell something stronger than formula. The kitten's kidneys, and maybe its bowels, were still working. Molasses stirred, and turned its head toward the eyedropper. It was sucking.

The movement woke Stacia, and she looked at the kitten.

"You're still hungry," she murmured. She fingered Molasses's back gently.

Ruth stared silently at the pair. There was more strength in them than she had planned on. But this miracle wasn't likely to last. Sooner or later, the kitten would start to fail, and what would Stacia do then?

A plan came to Ruth suddenly. There was another nursing cat in the barn that had only two kittens. A third one had recently died, and maybe the mother would accept this kitten as a substitute. It was a long shot, but no more so than trying to feed the kitten with an eyedropper.

"Stacia, we have another mother cat that's still nursing. Maybe she'd be willing to take care of this one. Cats really do take better care of their babies than we can."

Stacia looked stricken and clung a little tighter to the tiny black ball. But she was silent and compliant as Ruth gently carried the kitten to the barn. They searched for a while before they found Buffy and her kittens, because Buffy was a shy mother who moved her offspring frequently. That was how the third kitten had died: it was too close to the horses and had been trampled. Finally, Ruth located Buffy under the tractor, nursing her two-month-old kittens. She didn't turn away when Ruth laid Molasses next to her. Looking bewildered, Buffy sniffed the strange kitten and then began to lick it.

"That's a good sign," Ruth said. "She's taking care of it. Let's give her a little time, and see if she'll let it nurse."

"If she's a good mother and feeds it . . . we can try," Stacia said slowly. She was so serious, like an adult leaving her child with a new sitter. She wanted to sit and watch, but Ruth insisted they both leave, saying the mother needed to be left alone in order to adjust to the new situation.

For the next few days, Stacia often went to the barn, but couldn't find Buffy or Molasses anywhere. It was better this way, Ruth thought. Stacia would gradually accept the loss of the kitten without having to view its demise. Stacia retreated back into her polite but distant self, and halfheartedly let herself become involved in the other activities Ruth had planned.

Jess returned home Saturday, five days after Stacia's arrival.

"I left a message at the hotel about Stacia," Ruth said as she kissed him. "You were never in your room."

"I got the message that Tracie had an emergency, and you were keeping one of the kids. I didn't realize it was Stacia." He stared at the slender girl in the front yard playing croquet then looked back at his wife. "She's had a rough life."

"She's been tested. She doesn't have AIDS."

"Oh! Are they sure?"

"You sound like all the others Tracie talked about who are afraid of Stacia."

"I didn't mean it like that. The last I knew, her mother was a druggie and had passed on AIDS to her baby. AIDS is the leprosy of our day, isn't it? It's a scary label."

"And Stacia is marked by it for life."

"The sins of the fathers . . ." Jess murmured half to himself as he watched Stacia playing with the Hoagland girls.

"Mrs. Campbell! Can you come here? Stacia fell! We were climbing the tree—the tree you said we could climb—and Stacia fell." Laura Hoagland was running toward Ruth, and Stacia hobbled along behind her, leaning on Mary Hoagland's shoulder. Stacia was laughing. She couldn't be too badly hurt.

She sat down on the step, displaying a bloody knee.

"Here, Stacia, let me clean up that scrape." Ruth brought a pan of water and a washcloth and sat beside Stacia. "Just water isn't going to do much for all that pitch, though. You girls are covered with it." They all laughed together. Then Ruth's face froze. Jess was watching through the living room window, frowning as she washed Stacia's knee.

The fun of the moment was over. "I think all three of you could do with a bath. Stacia, take them to the bathroom upstairs." After they were gone, she went into the living room, where Jess was reading the newspaper. He stared at the page, avoiding her eyes.

"Stacia doesn't have AIDS, Jess. It isn't dangerous for me to wash her cuts."

He looked up from his paper and smiled sheepishly. "I know. It's just something I've got to get used to. I'm sorry."

"I know how you feel. Before she got here, I was so worried. Now I feel sorry for her. I guess that's why I let her fuss with that kitten." She told him about Molasses.

Jess shook his head. "Ruth, after going through it with our own boys . . . and it's worse for this poor kid, who's going to take that sadness back to her own sad life."

"I know. But Stacia wanted it so badly, saying no would have been worse than not trying."

"The kitten will not live. You've given up now, haven't you?"

"We tried something different. I gave her to Buffy to see if she'd nurse it. If the kitten is going to die anyway, how can that make it worse?"

"It could be worse for Stacia. Because Stacia is the real rejected baby, and she knows it."

"I think she wants to give the kitten a chance that she didn't have."

"And when she finds out she can't? What happens then?"

"I don't know. I don't know what happens when Nature's Law is applied to humans. You tell me, Jess."

Jess took her in his arms. "Humans get more chances than cats, Ruth. Let's keep hoping for her. Moses was pulled out of the Nile and saved. That's my Sunday school lesson for tomorrow, by the way."

"Well, I just remembered I have three girls to pull out of the water myself."

Before church, Jess went out to the barn to do the milking, and Stacia followed him. She was eager to see the barn cats come out to get a squirt of milk from him. Ruth had told Stacia about it the first time they went to the barn, but now Ruth wished she'd never mentioned it.

After Jess came back to the house, Ruth asked, "Did you see Buffy?"

"Yes, she came out. But her kittens weren't with her."

"None of them?"

"Ruth, it'll be a wonder if that scatterbrained cat doesn't let her other two kittens get kicked in the head, let alone that black runt."

"Oh, Jess, she's not that bad a mother. I hope you didn't say that to Stacia."

"No, I told her that the kittens were probably still sleeping."

"Good. Maybe she'll forget about Molasses."

Jess rolled his eyes as if to say, "Fat chance." But he worked as hard as Ruth in the next few days to occupy Stacia with other things. They went to a local circus on Sunday afternoon, and he took her down the road to the Hoaglands' to ride their pony. He even found time to join them when they went to the lake for a picnic.

On Wednesday, they got an unexpected call from Tracie. Her mother was healing more quickly than expected, and Tracie was bringing her home from the hospital. Also, Social Services had found a new foster home for Stacia. Tracie wanted to pick up Stacia and help get her established there.

Ruth dreaded telling Stacia about it. She tried to be enthusiastic, saying the new family had children her age, and an aboveground swimming pool. She needn't have worried. Stacia's reaction was surprisingly cheerful, even excited. She hugged Ruth, saying, "I'm going to miss you," and then set about the task of packing her bag without another sign of emotion. That must be how Stacia survived: form attachments quickly then give them up just as fast. Was there an "outgoing mail" slot somewhere in her soul where memories of loved kittens and people were dropped when she left them?

The only tense time was when Stacia asked to go out to the barn to say goodbye to the animals. She hadn't mentioned Molasses since the day they left the kitten with Buffy, but Ruth felt her heart go into her throat. She shot a look of panic at Jess, and he came to her rescue.

"I'm going out to the barn anyway," he said. "Come on, Stacia."

Ruth watched them nervously as they headed across the backyard. She had turned back toward the house when she heard a screech from Stacia. Oh don't have an accident now, she prayed, as she ran to the barn.

Stacia was coming toward Ruth, clutching her arm as if it

were hurt. Then Ruth saw she was gingerly holding an object across her chest.

"Molasses came to say goodbye!" Stacia was shouting. In disbelief, Ruth looked for evidence that Stacia was mistaken, that this was really another kitten. Its eyes were open now, bright blue and darting around at its world. In a moment, Buffy was at Stacia's heels, meowing worriedly. It was Molasses, all right. Stacia had Buffy's adopted kitten, and Buffy was upset.

Ruth laughed. "Buffy thinks you're trying to steal her baby. You'd better give it back."

Stacia put the kitten on the ground, and it ran to its mother, gliding between her legs. Buffy guided Molasses back toward the barn.

"We never found out if it's a boy or girl," Stacia said.

"Oh, we can find that out fast," Ruth said. Ignoring Buffy's dismay, she picked up the kitten and gave a quick look under the tail. "Molasses is a girl."

Stacia jumped up and down excitedly. "Molasses is a girl and she has a new mother. Sometimes babies can find new mothers."

Ruth choked up so fast, the only thing she could do was to grab Stacia and hug her tightly.

"May I come back and visit again?" Stacia asked.

"Of course, honey. We'd love to have you."

"Unless," Stacia said, "I get a new mother."

Ruth watched the little black kitten disappear into the barn with its mother. "Yes," she said. "That could happen."

The Freedom Quilt

by Lisa Barrick

CARRIE BINGHAM STEPPED outside to fetch the wash from the line. It was a warm fall afternoon, making it a real pleasure to be outside the dark, dreary cabin. Fall colors were dancing all around her. The fiery reds of the maples, the mellow gold of the oaks, and the evergreen of the cedars made her ache with the beauty. She paused at the clothesline, looking all around her, storing it up for those gray bleak days of winter that were not very far away. Then she would be shut inside the small cabin those short dim days with only the light of the fire and one small window to see by. So she would take every chance she could spare to step outside and breathe the clear clean air. Carrie reached for her son John's overalls. They needed to be patched yet again. She smiled to herself, thinking that he paid no mind to the reaching briars or grasping brambles. He would just pull free of them and keep on his way. She folded them and reached for her daughter Sarah's dress, the gingham color rapidly fading from the harsh lye soap Carrie used to wash. Sarah didn't mind. She understood pioneer ways, and a faded gingham dress was better than a flour sack dress. Carrie reached for her husband's overalls. They too needed some more carefully sewn patches. He worked many hours wrestling corn and wheat crops from the stubborn stony ground down behind the cabin, in the fields alongside the river.

Finally, Carrie reached for her quilt. Its worn edges warned that another washing would bring disaster, for its threads were raveling, its seams failing, and the colors fading. Carrie hugged the quilt to her, breathing the sunshiny smell that clung to it deep into her lungs. The pattern, a star, was done with many types of materials gleaned from years of collecting scraps of this and that. This pattern was very common in this part of the country. But Carrie smiled to herself as she wrapped her arms more tightly in the quilt. This quilt held many family memories, many stories. Her mind turned back to one of those stories, causing the sunshine to turn slightly chilly as she thought back. It was a day much like this one.

The day had dawned fair and bright and colorful. Carrie and Sarah had been harvesting the turnips, potatoes, and carrots from their spent kitchen garden, knowing that with winter hard on the heels of this late fall, the necessity of preserving every crop was of vital importance. God had blessed them with this later-than-usual fall. But Carrie didn't believe in taking God's provision lightly. She'd used the extra days He'd provided to store up their harvest with diligence.

She and Sarah had been singing at their work. Somehow the words and the tune made the work go more quickly and kept the aches in their bodies from being so noticeable. She had just heaped her washtub full with the last row of turnips when a man dressed in rough clothing had suddenly ridden through the trees. His horse was sweating and blowing, its hooves restless.

"Howdy, ma'am," the stranger called, tipping his hat. Carrie straightened up, rubbing her back and squinting in the sunshine at the newcomer. Folks riding in for a visit in the middle of the week weren't common. Not unless it was bad news. Or news of any sort out here in the Kentucky wilderness.

"Can I help you, sir?" she asked after a minute's hesitation.

The man climbed down from the horse and walked slowly toward her. His eyes were carefully studying her and Sarah. "I'm a friend of Joshua Rhodes," he said. There was a peculiar significance to his introduction.

Carrie's grip on the spade tightened. She turned and looked at Sarah. "Go on into the house and fetch a bit of that cornbread from this morning. This man looks like he could use a bit of something to eat."

"Yes, Mama," Sarah answered. She put down her hoe and walked toward the cabin. But she couldn't help looking back at her ma and the stranger standing there separated by the crooked rail fence.

Carrie fixed her eye on the man. "I was told you'd be coming."

"Yes, ma'am. And I was told that you would be willin' to help take care of a package for me every so often." He kept glancing around, toward the cabin, his eyes flitting over it, toward the barn, and then skipping along the back fence and over the cleared ground stretching out behind the cabin and toward the river. Finally his gaze came back and focused on her. "Is your husband . . . agreeable?"

She nodded with confidence. "Yes, he stands beside me."

The man nodded, with a fleeting smile on his face. "I wish we had more folks that were willin' around here." He heaved a sigh. "But we do with what we have."

"I reckon," Carrie agreed. This was all new to her. She only knew the barest details.

"I'll be bringin' a package down the river tonight," he told her suddenly.

Carrie was startled. She didn't think she'd be required of so suddenly. "The package . . ." the words were unfamiliar, the implied meaning alien to her. "Have they been told what to look for?"

"A quilt with a star design hanging out the window."

That was something she certainly could manage. But she felt she had to ask, "What else do I need to do?"

"A bit of straw to rest on, and some food and fresh water. Nothin' fancy. There's no time. The package will be picked up and dropped at the next station, 'bout ten miles from here."

That evening, the waning moon rose in the mist of passing clouds. It played hide-and-seek among the trees. Carrie sat knitting by the fire. Beside her was Joe, repairing a broken harness. He glanced up, his eyes questioning. An unspoken communication passed between them. What they were doing was right. Despite the danger it could bring to them, neither could sit by and let such a wrong continue if they in some minute way could change it. And Carrie knew that Joe felt just as strongly as she. He would stand by and support her. They had both spent hours in prayer, telling God about their mutual desire to do *something*. Ever since they'd heard about the Lincoln-Douglas debate and heard snatches of *Uncle Tom's Cabin* at church, they had questioned the so-called "institution of slavery." Carrie and Joe's voices had risen in their congregation when the debates over the practice were waged, both in the women's sewing circle and among the deacons. Weeks later, Carrie had been approached by an older church member after a church social. The woman had questioned Carrie closely. Satisfied with her answers, she told Carrie she would be contacted.

Carrie again checked the bundle of cornbread she had wrapped in a bit of towel. It was still warm; the comfort of it seeped into her hand. Food was hard to come by out here, but she had always been willing to share what little she had, no matter how meager or bland. The children were abed in the loft just over her head. They had been curious about the stranger who stood in the garden and talked to Mama. But they were good children, and did not question her. They trusted her judgment. Carrie wondered how far that trust would go after this night, should the secrets be told. Would they agree with their parents' decision to risk destroying the life they had always known? Those doubts quickly fled. Carrie smiled to herself. She had taught them that there were no differences in men or women. No matter the circumstances they lived in and no matter the color of their skin. All were the same in God's eyes. She and Joe could trust their children; she knew this with a mother's certainty.

There was a soft tapping at the door. Carrie glanced at Joe. He rose slowly to his feet, the harness hanging in his hand, and then dropping to the floor forgotten. Carrie crept to the door, opening it a crack. The familiar hat was the first thing she saw.

"Evening, ma'am," he said in a hoarse whisper. "I have three packages." He looked behind him in the darkness. Carrie strained to see, but the moon had slid behind a cloud and it was as pitch as the bottom of a well.

"I have to go, the paddy rollers were down the river a bit and I need to lead them away from this place." He jerked his thumb in the direction of figures she could not yet see. "They know where to go next," he told her. Then he turned from her door and spoke in a low voice to someone nearby.

Carrie opened the door just wide enough to let the three inside. They stood huddled together, their backs against the door, blinking fearfully at her and Joe. They were dressed in rags, their feet bare save for more rags tied around them. Their dark eyes were glazed with fear and fatigue. The look of the hunted marked each face.

"Please come to the fire, it's warmer," she coaxed gently, as if speaking to one of her children freshly wakened from a nightmare. Her soothing voice did its work and they moved as one creature to the comfort of the crackling fire. Carrie had a bucket of fresh water waiting to wash down with the warm cornbread. She approached them, bearing the offerings. At first, the three exhausted visitors just stared at her.

"Please, I fixed this for you," she told them in a murmur. "You must eat." Understanding dawned and the three nodded, reaching for the bread and water. Hunger made quick work of the bread. They carefully saved each crumb and finished it. The bucket stood empty.

The oldest of the three snatched the battered hat from his dark head. He crushed it in his strong worn fingers. He glanced up at Carrie, then at the floor, unable to look at her directly. "Thank ya, ma'am. Thank ya. We is beholden to ya for helpin' us."

Before Carrie could reply the sharp incessant barking of hounds pierced the darkness around the little cabin. The three figures froze, terror streaking across their faces, the fire reflected in their wide trembling eyes.

Joe was beside her. "The root cellar."

In a wink, he had the door open, hidden beneath a rag rug in the center of the room. The three fugitives tumbled into the dark hole, beside the vegetables. Carrie threw down another quilt, knowing it was chilly there in the dark confines of earth. Then Joe snapped the door shut, placing the rag rug just so as Carrie went to open the door.

The barking and yelping of the hounds in the yards scraped across already taut nerves. Joe stood beside her as she opened the door. The moon had fully risen now and the clouds had scudded away, revealing at least six mounted men. Moonlight glinted off their weapons and deepened the shadows of their faces, hidden beneath their hats. One man nudged his horse forward. The dogs frolicked through the yard, sniffing at every little thing.

"Sorry to bother you folks this night," the man said, his

voice coming from the abysmal darkness beneath his hat. It gave the impression of something evil speaking from the depths of Hades. Carrie suddenly realized the danger her family was in. Gooseflesh rose up on her arms. Instinctively, she knew this man could be trouble.

His name was Tip. He'd been out several nights like this before. He liked the shadowy woods, the comfort of the rifle slung across his saddle, the excited barking of dogs on a scent. He'd hunted through solitary forests and shadowy woods almost since he could walk. He could recognize the changing air when a storm was coming or sense when a huge buck stood in the cover of brush, trembling with the urge to run, its fierce proud heart rushing with fear. But the hunt for food was far from Tip's mind this night. This night he and his friends were after game that presented a challenge unlike any bear or wildcat they would ever encounter.

He leaned over his horse's neck, watching them. "We're on the trail of some runaway slaves. Three of 'em. And the no-good cusses who're helping them. Have you seen anyone tonight?" The other riders hung back, silent, waiting. Their horses shifted, their hooves stamping, their velvety noses snorting steam into the chill night.

Carrie felt as if she was being tested, her answers gauged carefully. She shook her head. "No, sir."

Joe echoed her words. "No, can't say as we've seen anyone tonight. We don't get too many visitors out here."

"Mind if we take a look around? Just to be sure no one is hiding out in yonder barn?" Tip asked with more than a hint of suspicion in his voice. People got strange notions, thinkin' they were doin' some good thing by hidin' stolen property.

Helping fugitive slaves would sometimes bring serious revenge. Lynch mobs made up of men who'd lost valuable property were not particular about destroyin' the property of those who'd helped the runaways. But he wasn't here to see that abolitionists were punished. No, he was here for the thrill of the hunt. The excitement throbbed in his veins hotly.

"There's nothing to see but an old cow, some shoats, and a broken-down mule," Joe told him firmly. His voice was cool and direct. His tone was clear in its meaning; there was no reason to search his property.

Carrie had a sense that this man would not be easily swayed into believing they had nothing to hide.

Tip shifted in the saddle. His horse pawed the packed dirt in the dooryard. Tip smiled with the leisurely smile of a cat that had cornered the weary mouse. "Well, see we was wonderin' 'cause we seen that you had a quilt thrown over the windowsill there. We've been told that's a sign. A sign for the runaways to look for, where folks will help 'em."

Carrie felt her heart shrivel up inside of her. Ice water seeped into her belly. In her haste to comfort the fugitives, she'd forgotten to remove the quilt. Now her foolishness would bring disaster to them all. She could feel Joe tense behind her. The night around them seemed to shrink and move in closer. Carrie could almost hear the terrified patter of the three hearts in the cellar just a few feet away. She could almost smell the sweat rolling from their bodies. Frigid sweat broke out over her own flesh.

"Why, I forgot I'd even put that there," she heard herself saying, like an addled and flustered girl. She walked over and balled it up over her arms. "I left that old quilt there 'cause I'd spilt water on it while I was carrying out the dishwater, and I wanted to see if it would dry before it got dark. I made this quilt for mine and Joe's weddin' and I use it on the bed every night. I didn't want to get any sparks from the fire on it 'cause it would ruin it for sure."

She had indeed sewn it for her dowry. Strangely enough, she had also spilled water on it while it was hanging there and she was carrying out dishwater. She'd hung the quilt intending to dry it and use it later. But in the rush to prepare for the strangers' coming, she'd forgotten. She thanked God for her clumsiness and His intervention. She wasn't telling a lie. The quilt was exactly where it needed to be.

Tip didn't speak for dragging moments. Then finally when he did it was with unmistakable warning, "If you see anyone that don't belong in these parts, you best be telling it or it will go poorly for you." With a shout he gathered the still yelping dogs and his fellow riders, wheeling their horses around. They left more quietly than they came, but the memory of their presence was not quickly forgotten.

Joe stood by the window to make certain they were gone. Carrie hurried to the trap door. She could smell the visitors' terror, but there was no way to imagine what they were feeling. To be pursued through the night, dogs snarling at their heels. The desperate runs through strange woods and unfriendly, unfeeling hearts chasing them, seeking reward.

They slowly crept up like the weight of dozens of years rested on them, visibly shaking with the nearness of their discovery. The one who had spoken before was trying to bring himself under control, but the silver tracks of tears glinted on his ebony skin.

"Ma'am, I cain't say how much we thank ya." He swallowed and continued, "But we best be goin'. We'll get up the river on our own."

Carrie was shaking her head, her own limbs quivering slightly. "No. I . . . we promised we would help. We have to wait another hour before the boat comes."

Joe turned from the window. "We gave our word."

"Mama?" The soft, questioning voice came from the loft. "Is something wrong?" Sarah started to climb down the ladder.

Carrie hurried to the foot of the ladder. "Nothing is wrong, Sarah. Go back to bed."

The three fugitives huddled beside the fire, too exhausted to move any further.

Sarah continued down. When she saw the three strangers, she gave a soft gasp. "Mama?" She knew that their being here had something to do with the man in the garden.

Carrie took her by the shoulders, her hands firm yet gentle. She looked intently at her daughter. "You understand what's happening? We're going to help these folks."

Wordlessly, Sarah nodded. She had a gentle heart and a discerning spirit. She knew.

John was down the ladder next, boots in hand. He'd been lying awake, listening when the dogs had barked the first time. He nodded to the strangers, giving them one of his quick, reckless smiles. Something about that smile put them at ease. John's smiles could instantly be trusted. Like his mother's.

"Does Pa need me?" He knew every creek, every fern-laden hollow on this land. There were many places that three people could vanish into if necessary.

Joe stepped closer to his family, his pride in them nearly choking the words from his throat. He looked at Carrie and saw the same pride, the same love. She smiled and nodded her approval.

Joe spoke quickly, "Go down to the river, son. To that shallow spot beneath that twisted oak. See if anyone is there. Be careful. Those men are likely still about."

John put on his boots and slipped out. Joe stepped just beyond the door to listen and watch.

Carrie and Sarah tended to the fugitives, bathing their weary bloody feet and tying clean rags around them. There were no shoes to be found for them but Carrie had plenty of quilt scraps. They would be put to better use now than in some fancy quilt she might never find time to piece. John's familiar whistle sounded from out of the darkness. Joe whistled back.

"The boat's here," he told Carrie. She was finishing tying the last bandage around one of the stranger's whip-scarred hands. Sarah was tying up a bundle of biscuits for them.

"It's time," Joe said as he stepped inside the cabin. The strangers rose to their feet still weary, but for the first time hope burned in their eyes.

The older man took Carrie's hands between his own work-gnarled fingers. "We cain't thank ya enough, ma'am. You an' your family. You've saved us. It's more 'n' any folk would do for the likes o' us."

She tightened her grip on his fingers. "It's not any more than our Lord asked us to do for our brothers."

He smiled and nodded, familiar with the passage. He'd heard it at his mother's knee, so very long ago and he quoted it with a soft, trembling voice. "Whatever you did for one of the least of these brothers of mine, you did for me" (Matthew 25:40).

The fugitives, after many days and nights of travel, made it to Indiana. Carrie and Joe Bingham, along with their children, helped nearly a dozen slaves to freedom in the North. For years after, when Carrie and Sarah would piece a new quilt, though they would try new colors and different patterns, there was one thing they never left out: the image of a star could always be found.

Restoration

by N. Miller Piper

SNIFFING AROUND MY backyard, hot on the trail of adventure, was a dog of questionable breed. He appeared to be a shepherd-collie mix, more shepherd than collie, except for the full waving tail that increased its tempo when he looked up at me. I bent to pet him and he sat on my foot. Looking from me, to the house, and back again, he whined softly.

Pulling my foot out from beneath him, I started toward the house, exhausted as always at the end of a long workday. My eyelids were heavy, and each step forward was an effort. I yawned extravagantly as I climbed the porch steps. Pausing, I looked back toward the dog. He stood staring at me. I turned, pulling open the screen door. That was when I saw that the window of the heavy wooden door had been broken. Fragments of glass crunched ominously beneath my feet. The lock on the door had been disengaged.

My pulse accelerated uncomfortably, apprehension replacing fatigue. I opened the door and entered the kitchen with bated breath. Flicking on the light, I saw that everything appeared to be as I had left it. If an intruder had indeed let himself into my home, he hadn't bothered to wash any of the dishes sitting dejected in the sink. The box of cereal was still on the table, beside a loaf of whole-wheat bread. I moved silently to the next room.

He was there, in my living room, one hand holding a pillowcase full of what were, no doubt, my belongings. His eyes bore into me, dancing eerily with the light from the kitchen. He appeared to be higher than a kite on a windy day, pupils dilated, eyes glassy.

I hoped he would turn, and perhaps make a run for the front door. Whatever was in the pillowcase didn't concern me in the least.

He started toward me, a crazy grin distorting his face.

I'm a large man, but so was this guy. Luckily, whatever drug was racing through his veins made him unsteady. Some animal cry escaped my lungs, and I met him head-on, giving him a shove that sent him reeling. He went down hard, taking a small end table with him. The pillowcase flew from his hand, landing with a clatter on the hardwood floor. He popped back up with amazing agility. Some black magic had placed a steel blade in his hand, and it glinted menacingly in the dim light.

In some dark recess of my mind, two things presented themselves: death was possibly looming on the forbidding tip of that knife, and, almost subconsciously, I heard the screen door squeak open and thud shut in the kitchen behind me.

The intruder lunged with murderous intent, knife looming large in slow motion. I braced myself for the inevitable pain, but it never came. A growling fury raced past me as a dog, the dog from the backyard, threw himself at my attacker, knocking him to the floor once more. The knife fell from his hand and slid, coming to rest at my feet.

The ensuing fight was a wicked flurry of fur, teeth, arms, and legs as the man tried to wrestle the dog from himself. The dog sunk in his teeth again and again as the man cursed and groaned. Ignoring the knife, I picked up a heavy lamp, which had fallen from the toppled end table, and brought it down hard on the man's head. He immediately went slack under the dog that held his arm tight within his jaws, growling and shaking his head violently from side to side.

"Stop!" I yelled. "Stop, it's okay, boy, he's out, stop!"

Finally letting go, the dog backed warily away, still growling. I quickly used the knife to remove the cord from the lamp then bent to tie the intruder's hands behind his back. Running to the kitchen, I grabbed the phone and dialed 911.

The police arrived with sirens wailing, piercing the quiet night, lights making crazy revolving patterns on the living-room walls. An officer replaced the lamp cord with handcuffs, and hauled the burglar away. Another put the knife in a plastic bag, and completed all the necessary paperwork.

I followed him to the porch, fresh air greeting me, soothing and cool. "We've had a couple other break-ins out this way," he told me. "Probably the same guy. Doesn't look like he did much damage to your home, but he *could've* done some damage with that knife. Good thing your dog showed up." He nodded appreciatively toward the dog that now stood at my side.

"Actually, he's not my dog. I really don't know where he came from. He was here, in the yard, when I came home. I've never seen him around, but I guess he's welcome to stay after what he did."

"Strange," said the cop, staring at the dog staring back at him. "I suppose you might want to run an ad looking for the owner. He'll need a license, and shots, in any case. Nice-looking dog . . ." The dog barked once, as if in agreement. The officer laughed as he started down the steps. "Take care," he called over his shoulder.

Beyond exhaustion, I turned, sweeping glass aside with my foot, and entered the house, locking the door behind me, despite the broken pane. The dirty dishes would wait another day. I headed up to bed, the dog following me.

I ran an ad, but no one called to claim him. Rambo, as I came to call him, greeted me ecstatically at the door each evening after work. He took up half the bed at night, but how could I turn him away? He was housebroken, well-mannered, and seemed quite fond of me, as if he'd known me his entire canine life.

I wondered about him. Where did he come from? I appreciated his timely appearance, but he was a mystery, and thinking too deeply hurt some inner part of me that was best left numb. He was welcome company, but I was weary and depleted.

The second Saturday after his arrival, I took him to the park in the early afternoon. I sat on a bench reading the newspaper, and he trotted around, sniffing every tree and bush in sight. I was engrossed in an article concerning the Middle East conflict and I lost track of him for a bit. He announced his return by nuzzling my arm with a wet nose, intent enough to knock the paper from my hand.

"Hello," said a small voice from behind him. A boy of perhaps five or six stood holding on to a fistful of Rambo's fur. Rambo turned and licked him. The boy laughed and said, "He missed me."

"He missed you?" I repeated. The kid was cute, bright-eyed, and all too present. His sandy blond hair was wind-blown in a disorderly fashion that somehow made him that much more appealing.

"He missed me. He found me. He was gone, but here he is." The boy smiled, tugging on Rambo's mane.

My heart, which I had believed was beyond danger of drowning, sunk into a murky pool of disappointment. "He's yours?" I asked with a forced smile.

The boy hugged the dog for all he was worth. Rambo grinned and waved his tail like a flag on the fourth of July. "Mine," he agreed. "He ran off awhile back, at night, all of a sudden. Mom said he was off on one of his missions."

"His missions?" I asked.

The boy adjusted the waist of his pants, which were a bit on the short side, white socks showing above torn sneakers, one lace tied, one dangling loose and frayed. "Yeah, he's run off before. He saved a little girl once. She fell in the river, and he swam out and got her. I was with him, so he followed me back."

"Back?" I repeated like an obtuse parrot.

"Back to my mom." He cocked his head to one side, lowered his eyebrows, and pushing his little face in front of mine, he narrowed his eyes. "He's trying to save *you*," he said in a knowing voice. "It's what he does."

His words made me flinch. I had heard them before, in another time, another place.

"He does . . . he did," I corrected, pulling back from the stare of this gnome in a red T-shirt with torn pocket. The dog, my dog, *his* dog, sat and stared intently into my eyes as though the command had been issued psychically from the gnome.

"Well," I breathed, a bit muddled under all this scrutiny, "I guess you found him, or he found you."

"Yep." The boy smiled happily at Rambo, who was almost at eye level with him. "Thanks, mister. I better go. Come on, Teddy."

Teddy. Rambo was a Teddy. Life might crush me, but it never failed to amaze me with its absurdity. Teddy. He whined a soft Teddy-style whimper, nuzzled me with his too-familiar wet nose, looked directly into my eyes, into my soul, barked twice in agitated farewell, turned, and followed the boy, banner still waving.

That night I saw the dog in my dreams. But as he crossed the street out of my life, it was Rachel who disappeared with him instead of the boy.

Rachel. More than six years had passed, and yet the aching wound she had left in my life still bled. Pouring myself into my job was therapeutic, and the pitcher ran dry most days, my arrival home accompanied by weary fatigue. How many nights had I slept deeply for a few hours, out of sheer exhaustion, only to awaken in the shadowed quiet of my room, unable to return to the balm of sleep? Life was an inexpressible burden without the woman I was born to love.

A tranquil beauty illuminated her face in the final moments. "You'll love again," she breathed, staring into my eyes.

"Rachel, no . . ." I began, trying valiantly to be brave, to hold it together for her sake. My hand clung desperately to hers, as if by sheer will I could keep her here with me.

"Yes, for me, you will. I can't bear to think of you alone. You're too good a man to be wasted." She smiled, her eyes shining with the light of heaven. "Someone out there will need you, and I'll be smiling down, so happy to know that your heart can still dance." She gave my hand a barely perceptible, encouraging squeeze. "Loving her will never take away what we've had. Promise me . . ."

"Rachel, I don't know if I can . . ."

"*I* know you can . . ." She turned her head away then, looking upward so intently that I followed her line of vision, trying in vain to see what she was seeing. "He'll save you . . . It's what He does."

She closed her eyes then, withered hand in mine. She slept, breath failing her, as did my resolve to be strong.

After Rambo, the return of silence was an unwelcome visitor, following me from room to room, making me uncomfortable in my own home. I returned to the park on Saturday afternoons, only subconsciously admitting that I hoped to see the dog once more.

Three Saturdays found me reading my paper peacefully,

no wet nose nuzzling me, no fuzzy head in my lap, no soulful eyes staring up at me. On the fourth Saturday of my vigil, I was deep into the sports section, when suddenly my paper imploded with the arrival of heavy panting; here, at last, was Rambo in all his wagging glory.

"Hey Bud, how are you?" I asked, matching his enthusiasm, giving his shoulders an affectionate shake.

In the midst of our reunion, I wasn't aware of the boy until he answered for the dog. "He's fine. Sorry about your paper. I guess he missed *you* this time."

"Well, *I* missed him. Has he saved anyone lately?"

"No, but he brought home a kitten with a broken tail. The vet took it off."

"Took what off?" Rambo, alias Teddy, rolled over on my feet, begging a belly rub.

"His tail. We named him Bob, because he has a bobtail."

I laughed. "A bobcat, huh?"

"Yeah, he looks kinda funny." He tipped his head to one side. "What's your name anyway?"

"My name's Jeff. What's yours?"

"I'm Alexander, but my mom just calls me Alex." He looked over at the swings, blowing in the wind, ghost children at play. "Hey, you wanna push me on the swing?"

Rachel and I had never had children, but she dearly longed for them. I knew she'd have found Mr. Alex to be quite charming. I smiled, rising from the bench, prompting Rambo to jump to his feet and follow us, tail swishing cheerfully.

Alex and I thoroughly explored the playground that afternoon. Lighthearted abandon washed over me, a feeling I'd not experienced in an eternity of dark, lonely days. So engrossed were we in our play that we didn't notice the darkening sky or lowering clouds until thunder rumbled in the distance. The wind picked up, scattering the paper I'd left near the bench. I hurried over to gather it up.

"Party's over," I said, surveying the rolling clouds. "Looks like a storm's brewing." As if on cue, the first pattering of sprinkles began to fall, quickly scenting the air with the aroma of freshly dampened soil. Lightning sliced the northern sky with sudden, vibrant energy. Alex cringed, his eyes growing large.

"Could you walk me and Teddy home?" He looked up appealingly. "*Pleease*?!"

I glanced toward my home, a block and a half away. Would Alex's mother and father appreciate a wet stranger bringing their child home? I hesitated, uncomfortable with the idea. Rambo-Ted paced between us, whining and panting hard in the stifling air.

"Okay, lead the way," I said finally. "Let's hurry."

Alex grabbed my hand, and together we trotted north through town, away from my house, into the storm, through streets blown clean of people, automobiles spraying rainwater behind them, wipers slapping. Thunder again issued its warning, as the day gave way to an alarming darkness.

The storm intensified rapidly, the tornado siren beginning an unholy rise and fall as the air became thick, a suffocating harbinger of trouble. Lightning cracked directly overhead.

"How much farther?" I yelled. My voice was tossed to the wind and lost. Rambo was in the lead, running ahead, nervously checking his shoulder to be sure we were following. I scooped up Alex in my arms, picking up speed, racing into the pelting rain.

Suddenly, I realized where we were going, and my heart sunk in dismay. We entered the trailer court, dashing beneath a large sign boasting SHADY RETREAT, which was bucking wildly in the wind. Despite its name, there was not a tree in sight, and the wind raged through the place, rocking the small homes in a frenzied rhythm. Debris began to fly, as though brought to life, swirling around us dangerously.

Alex put his arms tight around my neck, pulling himself up to my ear. "Go to the office building!" he screamed. "There's a shelter, a basement!"

I struggled forward as the rain changed to hail, clanging off the swaying trailers, stinging our skin like a swarm of furious hornets. Reaching the building, I set Alex down and wrestled with the door. The wind tore it from my hands as it finally shot open. Rambo burst in ahead of us. We raced for the storm shelter stairs, sodden, muddy, and breathless.

The murmur of apprehensive voices greeted us.

"Alex!" a woman's voice cried out. "Thank God!" She rushed forward, dropping to her knees to embrace him. Tears of relief streamed down her face. Rambo shook himself hard, mud flying. "Teddy," she laughed. He licked her face, banner waving, smiling his adoration.

From her position on the floor, still holding Alex in a steel grip, she looked up at me with a million questions in her deep brown eyes. Slowly she came to her feet, reaching out a slender hand.

"Hi, I'm Kaitlyn, Alex's mom."

Her smile was the sweetest thing I'd seen in years.

Like Rachel, Kaitlyn's husband had died of cancer. A widow for four of Alex's six years, she struggled to make ends meet, waitressing at a local upscale restaurant. She hoped to become a writer of children's books, pursuing her passion every precious spare moment, with cheap spiral notebooks and expensive pens.

The tornado had cut a zigzag course through town, destroying some buildings and completely missing others. Trees were uprooted, cars overturned. The trailer court was devastated. Kaitlyn dug through the wreckage with frenetic energy, finally uncovering her notebook, which was somewhat damp and tattered but still intact. Alex uncovered a framed photo of his father, which was amazingly unspoiled. He hugged it to himself protectively, then wrenched a large soggy cushion from the debris.

"Teddy's bed," he said in a subdued voice. A plaintive meow marked the return of the bobtailed kitten. "Bob!" shouted Alex.

They had nowhere to go. An only child, parents deceased, estranged family out of state, Kaitlyn was at a loss. I took them into my home that evening, all at once grateful to be alive. Mother and son disappeared into the bathroom for a full hour, while I changed my clothes and washed up in the kitchen sink. Alex came out, dressed in a towel, to retrieve their freshly laundered clothes, and soon they emerged, smelling of soap and looking refreshed. The kitten trailed behind them, playfully batting a bottle cap with its paw.

Kaitlyn smiled uncertainly. I knew how vulnerable she must feel in the home of a man she barely knew, despite the fact that Teddy obviously approved of the arrangement. Curled in front of the fireplace, where flames leaped and danced, his paws twitched merrily as he chased rabbits through an ethereal forest.

Kaitlyn's golden brown hair shined around her delicate features. She folded her arms nervously in front of her, surveying the room. She paused wistfully when she saw my computer, no doubt wondering about its word processing ability.

"Have a seat." Guiding her to the sofa, I took a chair across from her. Alex joined us and we talked, quickly at ease with one another. There was an enormous sense of peace after such a turbulent day.

Kaitlyn and Alex sat captivated as I related the story of the burglary and Teddy's heroism that night. I listened to a multitude of stories about the dog who had whisked in out of nowhere to save my life. Two hours passed. We laughed, we cried, we warmed to one another like survivors of a cold desolate journey through the barren landscape of loneliness.

Alex brought us back to reality.

"I'm starving," he groaned.

Some people call it destiny. Some call it fate, karma, chance, luck . . . I choose to call it God.

One month after these beautiful people moved into my life, we became a family. The wedding was simple, but my heart was indeed dancing, as Rachel had predicted. The freedom to love, to reach tentatively for life once again, was her gift.

The night before Kaitlyn, Alex, Teddy, Bobtail, and I were married, I found myself alone in the bedroom, the room I would soon share with Kaitlyn. I prayed for the first time in six long years. I realized, deep in my soul, that my greatest loss had been the loss of my faith. A chasm had been cut, with razor sharpness, straight through my heart, leaving me wounded and bleeding, with no lifeline.

I took Rachel's favorite Bible down from the shelf, wiping dust from the worn leather cover. I thumbed idly through the pages, marked and highlighted in her search for truth. A small note card in a bright yellow envelope fell to the floor. My breath caught when I saw my name written in her tidy script.

I picked up the note and sat on the bed, the bed we had once shared. With trembling fingers, I opened it.

> *Who, O God is like you? Though you have made me see troubles, many and bitter, you will restore my life again; from the depths of the earth you will again bring me up.*
>
> *Psalm 71:19-20*

Jeff,

 I know how deeply you grieve, and how lost you must feel. But you mustn't close your heart to God. Remember, He loves you, even more than I do, if that is possible. I want so much for you to be happy. He will work to restore you, and your life. Please let Him. I love you.

 Even now.

Rachel

We celebrated Alex's seventh birthday on February seventh, exactly seven years after Rachel's death; the child destined to become my son was born on the day that Rachel passed away—both events in the same hospital. We were all there on that significant day, a day of joy, a day of sorrow.

All except, of course, Teddy. *He* arrived at Shady Retreat the evening of the same day: hungry, dejected, no collar, no home.

Kaitlyn's husband took him in, believing that, in time, every kindness would be rewarded.

Love on the 4:52

by Carrie Turansky

THE FIRST NOTE appeared in my lap one rainy afternoon as I rode the 4:52 train home from work. I didn't see it until I pulled my gaze from the rain-spattered train window to prepare to get off at my stop. I'm not really surprised I missed seeing who'd dropped it there. I'd been crying most of the way home from Philadelphia. That afternoon I'd found out I'd been passed over for a promotion at work, my sister called to cancel her upcoming visit, and worst of all, my dog Hemmingway had been missing for two days. Curious about where the note came from, I glanced around the car. No one looked my way. Some read novels or the newspaper, others worked on laptops or slept, and a few simply stared out the window lost in their own world, as I had been moments before.

I looked at the note in my hand. Who would pass me a

message on a commuter train? I slowly unfolded it. Before I read the message, the strong, neat handwriting gave the impression the author was a male with an artistic bent.

> I see you crying. I'm sorry you're hurting. Don't give up. Things will get better. I'll be praying for you.

> R.

I blinked away a fresh round of tears, and read the note once more, savoring each caring phrase. Then I carefully refolded it, and slipped it into my coat pocket. Someone saw and cared. Someone prayed for me. I smiled, and felt my spirit lift.

The following afternoon, I dashed around the puddles and prayed I'd make the 4:52. Hemmingway was still missing, but things were looking more positive at work. As I took my usual seat in the third row from the front, a young woman with long red hair sat down next to me. We were soon laughing and sharing war stories about working in downtown Philly. I even showed her the note.

As I smiled and waved goodbye to her, someone tapped me on the shoulder. I turned, and an older gentleman handed me a note. I stared at him, and he chuckled. "Don't look so worried. It's not from me. Someone passed it up from the back."

"Thanks," I mumbled, blushing, and accepted the second note.

Glad to see you smiling today. I guess you must be feeling better. See, prayer works. I hope you have a nice weekend. I'll keep praying for you.

Your Commuter Prayer Buddy,
R.

At the bottom he'd sketched a drawing of me smiling. I laughed softly, looking at the sketch. It was surprisingly good. Then I read the note again before I folded it and hid it in my pocket along with the first.

On Monday, I stopped to check my hair and makeup before I made the mad dash for the 4:52. Thirty minutes later, as we crossed the river into New Jersey, I sunk lower in my seat and sighed. No note. No message. Nothing. Where was R.?

Only two minutes from my station, I grabbed a blank piece of paper from my bag and quickly scribbled a message.

Dear R.,

Thanks for your notes and prayers. Most people are too wrapped up in themselves to notice anyone else. I do believe in prayer. I appreciate the reminder that I can always take my problems to the One who is never too busy to listen. I had a good weekend. I found my dog Hemmingway! He's been lost for six days. I'm sure that's partly due to your prayers. I'll say a prayer for you too.

Lisa, your friend on the 4:52

As the train pulled to a stop, I hesitated, feeling silly. Would he get the note? I had to try. I quickly wrote: *To R. on the 4:52.* Several people stared at me as I attached the note to the window with an old sticker from my purse. With flaming cheeks, I made a quick exit, feeling both foolish and hopeful.

Over the next two weeks we exchanged several other notes, each one revealing a little more. But this note changed everything.

> Lisa,
>
> This all started because I saw you crying and wanted to help. But, over the last few weeks I've become very intrigued by you. I would like to meet you and have a chance to get to know you, but there is no pressure from me. If you're married or dating someone else, I understand. This will be my last note. If you'd like to meet, then ride the 4:52 tomorrow.
>
> Ray

I bought a new blue sweater on my lunch break, and I watched the clock all afternoon. I left work at exactly 4:30, but a fire across from my building closed the street and I had to run three blocks out of my way.

I missed the 4:52, and missed my chance to meet Ray. Tears blurred my eyes as I boarded the 5:03 and fought off a miserable wave of hopelessness. I excused myself up the crowded aisle looking for a vacant seat.

When I reached the third row, I stopped and stared. A dozen red roses lay in my seat. A handsome man with wavy dark brown hair sat in the aisle seat next to mine. He wore a charcoal business suit with an eye-catching red tie.

I smiled, hope rising in my heart. "Excuse me. Is that seat taken?"

He glanced at me, and a slight smile lifted the corners of his mouth. "Well, I was saving it for someone." I nodded, suppressing a giggle. "But she's late . . . so would you like to sit down?" His brown eyes danced with amusement.

"Yes, thanks."

He reached for the roses, then stood and moved into the aisle. For a moment we stood face to face, smiling into each other's eyes. "When you didn't get on the 4:52, I took a chance and waited for the 5:03." Ray handed me the roses.

My smile spread wider, and I hoped it would express what my words could not. I lifted the bouquet to my nose and inhaled their sweet scent. "Thank you. They're beautiful."

We sat down together in the third row, and we laughed and talked all the way home to New Jersey.

The Arrangement

by Tina Helmuth

M ARY STARED AT the coins in her hand, as though they would multiply if she looked at them long enough. She was holding her income for the week and it wasn't enough to buy flour and oil for bread. One meal's worth of bread remained in her cottage, and then she would have nothing but fruit to eat. She had already tried hiring herself out as a servant, but no one had any positions available. Selling fruit from her own small orchard had been her last option. *Maybe things will be better next week*, she thought. But that hope was wearing thin.

Tears blurring her vision, she didn't see the old man sitting beside her stall until she nearly tripped over him. One of his arms was raised in a pleading gesture, his sleeve hanging in tatters. He was so thin that his hand looked too big for his arm. Dirt streaked his face and one eye was milky with blindness. Mary blinked back her tears in shame. What did she have to complain about? She had a roof over her head and at least something to eat every day. She silently thanked God for the reminder to be grateful for what she had.

"Come with me," she said. "I will share my supper."

The beggar tilted his head to consider her with his good eye. "I be too weak to walk."

"Then take this," she said, splitting open a soft melon and handing it to him, "and I'll be back later with some bread."

"Bless you, child," he said with wonder on his face.

From a nearby carriage, a richly dressed man had been watching the scene. "She's the one," he said.

"Her? She's nothing but a street waif!" his servant protested in a disbelieving tone.

"She's the one," he repeated firmly. "Follow her."

At the sound of footsteps behind her, Mary quickened her pace. *A clumsy thief this one is. Or is he so confident he has no need to mask his steps?* Whichever it was, Mary couldn't allow another barrow of fruit to be stolen, and the footsteps were coming faster now. Taking a better grip on the handles of her cart, Mary ran as fast as her burden would allow.

"Please, Miss, wait!"

Please, Miss? If a clumsy thief was rare, a polite one was unheard of. She chanced a look over her shoulder. The fine fabric of the man's clothing told her he was no thief, so she stopped. Clutching his side, the little man took a moment to catch his breath before giving what sounded like a memorized speech.

"I am Mr. Pensington, personal attendant to Mr. Robert Talsleigh. My master is very old. He regrets never having married. He wants a wife to take care of him until he passes on, and he has chosen you. You'll be a wife in name only." At that Mr.

Pensington simply stopped talking and waited for her reply.

Mary stared at him, uncomprehending. "I beg your pardon?"

With a sigh, he began again, slowly annunciating. "I am the personal attendant of—"

"No," she stopped him. "I heard everything you said, but it's not making much sense. My cottage is just around the corner. Perhaps you'd better come in and explain."

"Very well." He reluctantly followed her.

Mr. Pensington gave her cottage a disdainful sweeping glance, and Mary found herself seeing it through his eyes. The floor was dirt, the walls needed replastering, and sky shone through holes in the roof's thatching. Clearing her throat uncomfortably, she asked, "Won't you sit down?"

He wrinkled his nose at the bench she indicated. "I prefer to stand, thank you."

Mary bristled. Meager though her possessions were, she kept everything spotlessly clean. "What did you mean when you said that your employer has chosen me for a wife?"

"Apparently Mr. Talsleigh has grown tired of the impersonal servants who wait on him. As his death nears, he wishes for family around him. Since he has none, the best he can do is take a wife."

"Why me? I've never met him." Everyone in town had heard of the wealthy Robert Talsleigh, who had a reputation for being eccentric, but few had ever seen him.

"I assure you," he said dryly as his glance fell on her patched dress, "I cannot fathom his reasons."

"What would be expected of me?" She found herself wanting to accept just to spite the stuffy little man.

"You will serve him meals, read to him, and keep him company when he so desires."

"You said a wife in name only?"

"Yes. He is bedridden and frail. Simply perform the duties I mentioned and you will be well taken care of."

"What do you mean by 'taken care of'?"

"You'll live in his luxurious manor, be given new clothes, and have plenty of the richest foods to eat."

It finally dawned on her that this was a way out of poverty and almost certain starvation. Her mouth was already watering at the thought of a real meal. She reminded herself that she was a businesswoman, and she mustn't jump at this proposal like a dog over a scrap of meat. "And after your employer dies, what happens to me?"

Mr. Pensington hesitated, and Mary got the impression that she had deviated from his rehearsed conversation. "I'm sure something will be arranged."

She was put off by his ambiguous reply, but even if her stay at the manor was temporary, what better offer was she likely to get? She had always had faith that God would take care of her. "I accept."

"Very well," Mr. Pensington said with a slight downturning of his lips.

Hearing a knock, Robert Talsleigh settled back into his bed and pulled the covers up to his chin. At his call, Pensington entered. He was alone and wearing his usual disapproving frown. "Well?" he prompted, looking for the girl.

"She accepted. She's waiting in the hall."

"Sir, if I may, it's not too late to end this foolishness. I can send her away with a handsome reward for her trouble."

"What's bothering you?" Robert didn't bother to mask his irritation and impatience.

"As soon as the girl realized she'd be the lady of the manor she started giving orders."

"Orders?" That didn't match his initial impression of her.

"Yes. She ordered me to help her carry the old beggar back to her cottage." Pensington gave an affronted sniff at the memory.

"How unseemly!" he said drolly. He was even surer of his choice. She hadn't forgotten the beggar in all the excitement. "Bring her in."

Mary stood admiring the delicate tapestries, silks, silver candlesticks, and the exotic vases and ornaments that lined the hall. Her eyes traveled along the plush rug until they reached her own dingy, worn shoes. Struck by the contrast, she had a strong urge to turn and run. She didn't belong in this place. But just then Mr. Pensington opened the door he had disappeared behind and beckoned to her. She slowly went forward into the room. A frail-looking man was lying in the bed, his face almost as white as his hair. He appeared to be sleeping and she was frightened at how near to death he seemed. Then he opened his eyes and she saw his lively blue eyes shining up at her. All at once she didn't feel quite so afraid, or out of place.

"What is your name, my dear?"

"Mary."

"Lovely." He gestured to a side door, and when Mr. Pensington opened it, a minister entered the bedroom. Mary blinked in surprise. She was directed to stand beside the bed and the man took her cold hand in his warm soft one. Before she could have second thoughts, the minister was pronouncing them man and wife.

"Now, my wife, I must rest. Go with Mrs. Grove."

A plump older woman appeared at the same door the minister had come through. Mary followed her through a sitting room to another bedroom. The woman told her where to find her new clothes and informed her that supper was in an hour. "You'll have time to change."

After Mrs. Grove left, Mary looked down at her dress. The dreadful thing had been her wedding dress! She had always hoped to be married in a nice dress, but then nothing about her wedding had been as she dreamed. She was married to an old man, a stranger. She leaned back against the door as her strength left her. *What have I done?*

By the time Mrs. Grove's polite knock announced supper, Mary was dressed in a gown finer than anything she'd ever seen. The shoes pinched her feet, but she felt like a lady.

"My, don't you look lovely!" Mr. Talsleigh exclaimed when he saw her. Then his brow creased. "I'm sorry. I should have let you change before the ceremony. How thoughtless of me."

"Not at all, Mr. Talsleigh."

"Call me Robert, my dear. I have servants to call me Mr. Talsleigh or sir. Remember, you're my wife." He smiled impishly and his blue eyes danced.

The irresistible aroma of the stew set before her caused Mary's stomach to rumble loudly. She blushed.

"A hearty appetite is nothing to be embarrassed about, my dear," he laughed. "Eat, eat!"

So Mary ate the delicious stew and soft bread with cheese, feeding her husband between her own mouthfuls. She could scarcely believe that she was able to eat until she wanted no more.

A knock woke Mary in the morning. "Time to get up," Mrs. Grove said, entering with a pitcher of hot water. "You must be ready to bring the master his breakfast."

"Thank you," she said. "If I want to go into town, who shall I ask to take me? Or shall I walk?" The old beggar had been on her mind all night. She had the feeling she should have done more for him than provide him with a leaky roof over his head.

"Town? You can't leave the property, madam. Didn't Pensington tell you? You must stay on the grounds at all times, to be near if the master calls."

"Oh," Mary said, surprised. "No, he didn't tell me."

"Rather an important bit for Pensington to leave out, if you ask me."

Mary agreed, but she didn't say so. She wondered if that would have made any difference in her decision.

Breakfast was a somber affair. Mr. Talsleigh was too weak for much talk and Mary's mind was too preoccupied to let her enjoy the food. She could see her days stretching out before her, filled only with feeding him bite after bite, meal after dreary meal. What a fancy prison she had chosen for herself! *Isn't anything better than starving to death?*

After the last bite of porridge was gone, she looked at the window and saw the sunlight struggling to filter in through the heavy drape. *Maybe the sunshine will cheer me.* Drawing back the drape, she gasped at the sight that met her eyes. A beautiful garden lay below her window, glowing in the late morning sun. It was an Elizabethan garden, if her memory served, and the vibrant colors beckoned to her.

"Is there anything else you need, Mr. Tal— I mean, Robert?"

"No. I can see that you're impatient to be off somewhere else." He looked hurt.

"Oh, I hope I haven't offended you. It's only that . . ."

"You're very young, and I'm very old."

". . . I would like very much to see the garden."

His childlike grin was back. "Is that all? Go and see it, but come back soon. I want us to talk and get to know one another."

"Yes, sir. Thank you."

Mary stopped several yards short of the garden. A tall hedge was blocking her way. Where was the entrance? Then she saw the archway cut into one end of the hedge and realized the hedge was hollow, like a tunnel. With a squeal of delight, she headed for the entrance.

What fun it was to walk inside the hedge, where the light was dimmed and the heat of the day was cooled. Evenly spaced "windows" in the hedge allowed her to look out into the garden occasionally. She came to another archway that led into the garden, and she stepped into enchantment. The garden was a feast for all of her senses, which had been so long deprived of anything beautiful. Along with the aroma of the flowers, the sweet scent of watermint and chamomile greeted Mary on the grassy path. She inhaled deeply, wondering where the scent was coming from, then saw that the herbs were planted in the grass of the walk and the scent was released by her footsteps.

The path divided the square garden into four plots. In two of the plots roses, marigolds, daisies, and violets were all planted together in a riot of color. The other two plots contained knot gardens, providing a dark contrast. She walked to the fountain in the center of the garden, whose splashing water had called to her, and absorbed the loveliness all around her. As long as she could come to the garden every day, she was sure she could be happy here. She would never tire of the splendor that was making her heart sing.

"It's so beautiful," she said aloud.

"Thank you!"

Mary jumped and turned to see a man weeding a flower bed.

"I'm sorry to startle you. I thought you knew I was here."

"Talking to myself is a habit I've picked up from living alone too long. Do you take care of all this?"

The man stood and wiped his hands on a handkerchief, smiling at the awe in her voice. He was a very handsome young man, with dark, wavy hair and big, brown eyes. "Yes. Although lately it's been an unnoticed labor. I'm glad someone can appreciate the garden again, besides me and God."

"I never thought of God enjoying a garden."

"He created this beauty, why shouldn't he enjoy it?"

Mary smiled. His lovely eyes had captured her; she couldn't look away. "You're right. Anyway, your labor won't go unnoticed as long as I'm here," she said, then flushed as she realized her words could be misinterpreted. "I'm sure I'll be spending a lot of time in the garden," she clarified. His smile widened, and Mary felt her belly going to liquid.

"You fit in this garden, somehow. It's as if it was made for you. I shall call you the Lady of the Garden. I'm Timothy," he said, holding out his hand.

She stood and shook his hand, noticing that he was tall and broad-shouldered. "I'm married." She saw Timothy's eyebrows go up in surprise. "I'm Mary. I meant to say that I was married to Mr. Talsleigh yesterday."

"Yes, I know. The whole town is talking about it. Mr. Talsleigh would be pleased to know his legend of peculiarity has grown."

"Are you often in town?" she asked, an idea flashing in her mind.

"Every few days."

"May I ask a favor of you?"

"Of course, my lady."

She smiled at his teasing use of the title. "When I came here, I let an old beggar have the use of my cottage. He was very weak, and I would like for someone to look in on him and bring him food. I would do it myself, but I'm not allowed to leave the property."

"You can't leave?"

"Mr. Talsleigh might call for me at any time, and he would be upset if I didn't arrive promptly."

"I would be, too," the man said with a grin and an appealing tilt of his head.

She lowered her eyes. "My cottage is out of the way, and I know this is a lot to ask."

"I will gladly do this for you."

"Oh, thank you!" she said, then was embarrassed at her

exuberance. "I'd better be going. I said I wouldn't be long."

With his pruning shears, Timothy began cutting some long-stemmed roses. "Take these with you," he said, looking deeply into her eyes. "It's a shame to keep such beauty confined to one place."

Mary held her vase of roses as she sat in her window seat two days later. Breathing in their rich fragrance, she couldn't help but smile, thinking of the charming man who had given them to her. Her smile faded. "I'm a married woman," she told herself sternly. She had to keep reminding herself of that, for although she was becoming fond of him, Mr. Talsleigh seemed more like a grandfather to her than a husband. Looking up from her flowers, she saw Timothy in the garden. She quickly went to see him, telling herself that she was only anxious for news about the beggar.

"How is he?" Mary asked after her greeting.

"He couldn't lift himself out of bed. He's been too long without nourishment. Now food alone may not be enough."

Mary nodded. She had feared that was the case.

"I asked the doctor to check on Jem—that's his name."

"Thank you," Mary said, troubled. "I wish I could have helped him."

"You have helped. He was grateful for what you did. He wanted me to thank you."

"But it wasn't enough."

"He's comfortable, has a roof over his head, and good food to eat. He may yet recover, my lady."

"Please, don't call me that. You saw where I lived. I'm no lady."

"Yes, you are a lady," he said earnestly. "A great lady."

Mary felt a lightness in her chest. She looked into Timothy's warm eyes and wanted to stay lost in them, where she could forget everything—forget that she had impulsively married to escape poverty, and given up her freedom for a life of ease.

The next week, Mary was kneeling by one of the flower beds, pulling weeds. She found herself with more free time than she knew what to do with so decided to help with the garden, where she had some experience. Suddenly she gasped as she felt a sweetbriar thorn bite into the flesh of her hand. In her shock, she snatched her hand back and the thorn broke off. She turned her palm toward herself and saw the end of the thorn sticking out of the deep puncture wound in the heel of her hand. A bead of blood pooled and trickled down her arm. She just stared at it.

Timothy had heard her pained cry and was instantly by her side. He gently cradled her hand in his. "This looks bad. I should have warned you about the thorns near this bed."

"I'm used to tending fruit trees. They don't have thorns." As the blood seeped into her sleeve, she was glad she had worn her old dress.

Timothy turned her hand this way and that, inspecting the thorn. "There is just enough left sticking out for me to get a grip on, but this is going to hurt."

She pressed her lips together and braced herself, then nodded that she was ready. Even so, she couldn't stop the cry that came from her lips as he pulled out the thorn in one smooth, swift yank. Timothy then took out a clean handkerchief and wrapped it around her hand.

"Keep pressure on it until it stops bleeding."

She nodded, drawn as always to his eyes. She was amazed

at the gentleness in his strong hands, and realized it had been a long time since she had been taken care of. After her parents had died, she'd had to fend for herself. Now she was taking care of an elderly man, her husband.

She had never given much thought to marriage, simply trusting that God would send the right kind of man her way when the time was right. Here she was, staring him in the face, but it was too late. Had she stepped outside of God's will when she married? She had thought it was God's provision for her, but the feelings that stirred when Timothy had touched her hand made her wonder. What kind of cruel trick was it that she should meet such a man only after she was married? Had she made a sham of God's holy institution of marriage by marrying for convenience? She hadn't even asked if he was a God-fearing man before she married him. It turned out that he was, but she had acted without knowing that. She hadn't taken the time to fully seek God's will.

She thanked Timothy and went back to the house.

"Mary, my dear," Robert called as she passed his doorway. "Back from the garden so soon? Come sit with me." She sat in the chair beside his bed. "I don't like to see you cooped up in the house so much. Why did you come in so soon?"

She held up her hand with its blood-soaked bandage. "The thorns sent me in early."

"How dreadful," Robert pursed his lips in sympathy and kissed the tips of the fingers of her injured hand.

Mary smiled.

"What's so amusing?"

"It's just that sometimes you're so . . ." she trailed off, afraid of offending him.

His eyes sparkled. "I'm so what?"

"Childlike."

Robert grinned. "Of course I am. I may have missed much by not having a family—I'll never know. But I do know this; since I never had children of my own, I never had to stop being a child. I rather like that."

Mary smiled and lightly touched her lips to the old man's forehead.

Timothy began making daily visits to Jem, so every day Mary would go to the garden to hear how the beggar was faring. Although she was genuinely concerned, she knew it was more than news of Jem that drew her to the garden day after day. She was troubled by her growing feelings for Timothy, yet was reluctant to rob herself of the pleasure of his company.

"And how is Jem today?" she called in greeting one cloudy day. "Did he like my lentil soup?"

Timothy looked down at the ground for a long moment before meeting her eyes. "I'm sorry, Mary. Jem passed on during the night."

Mary's hand flew to her mouth in shock. "I'd just begun to hope that he'd get better." She was surprised to find her eyes filling with tears, not realizing she had cared so deeply. Jem had been her only contact to the outside world these past weeks. He had become her purpose, her means of passing along the good fortune that had come to her.

"You gave him a measure of happiness before he died. He once told me that he was ready to leave this world, knowing that there were still kind people in it."

Hearing that she had meant so much to Jem only made his

loss hit harder. She covered her face with her hands. Timothy put his arms around her and she leaned into him, grateful for the comfort of the man she loved. Mary stiffened in shock and pushed away from him. Love? Yes, she loved him. And from the look in Timothy's eyes, she knew he felt the same way. It couldn't be. It *mustn't* be. She fled.

"You're beginning to look as pale as I, young lady," Robert gently scolded. "Get some sunshine. Go to the garden. I know how you love it."

"Later." She'd been avoiding the garden for days, avoiding the temptation to give in to her feelings. "Shall I start another book?"

"No, I think I'll nap now. Go to the garden. That's an order," Robert said, attempting to look stern. "Bring back some roses. This room needs color. Make it two bouquets, just to be sure you get enough fresh air."

Since she couldn't give him a reason for a refusal, Mary obeyed. She hoped Timothy wouldn't be there, but he was a conscientious gardener.

"I'm thinking of planting more flowers," Timothy said, keeping his tone casual. "I thought hollyhocks might be nice. What do you think?"

"That would be lovely," she said absently, not really hearing his words.

"Or maybe some thistles and burs?"

"Yes," she said.

"No, I think I'll go with stinkweed. You don't want a garden smelling too nice, after all."

Again she agreed. Timothy laughed, and when the meaning of his words registered, she smiled.

"You're unhappy," he said, growing serious.

"Oh, no. Not really," she said, clipping the roses faster.

"You are. I can see it in your eyes." He spoke with sudden fire. "You shouldn't be married to a dying old man. You deserve to have someone you can love, not just care for, and who loves you in return."

She looked up at him in surprise. "Please don't." She could deny the feelings between them, as long as they weren't spoken of.

"Mary, I love you." She closed her eyes at the bittersweet sound of those words and rose to leave, but he grabbed her arm. "I'm leaving here."

The words made an impact she could feel in her stomach, but she said, "I suppose that's best."

"Come with me."

She gasped at his boldness. "How could I?"

"I love you, Mary. You love me, too, don't you?" His eyes searched hers. "Don't you?"

"Yes, I do," she said and Timothy smiled in triumph. "But I'm married. How could I turn my back on Robert? He's been so kind."

"You're a maid, not a wife. Just walk away."

"Why can't you stay here? He's dying. With a little patience, we could be together." Mary was appalled at how callous she sounded. "I didn't mean—"

"He's been on his deathbed for months! And this isn't the first time he's taken to his bed. He's always gotten better, and this time may be no different. It could be years. I can't wait that long." He released her arm. "And I can't stay here knowing we love each other, but can't be together."

Mary sat on a bench and dropped her head into her hands, distressed at the thought of losing him. But, given the circumstances, that's how it had to be. "I can't go with you."

"Is it because of the money? I happen to know that when Talsleigh dies they'll throw you out on the streets. You won't see a penny. You'd be better off coming with me now."

"It's not about money." How could he think her so petty? "I never thought I would leave this house with any more than I brought with me. It's about integrity. I'm his wife."

"Wife. That's just a name he calls you. I would treat you as a wife should be treated." He pulled her to him for a kiss, but she turned her face away and broke free.

"No, not just a name. It's a promise! I made my vows before God. They're sacred, and I can't break them. If you can't see that, you aren't who I thought you were." She turned her back resolutely and walked away, paying no heed when he called her name. She retreated to her room where she could be alone with her tears. Knowing she'd done what was right gave her little comfort.

A knock on the door interrupted her thoughts. She wiped her eyes before calling, "Come in."

"The master needs you, madam," Mrs. Grove spoke urgently. "Right away."

Mary quickly went to Robert's room, but hesitated at the door, afraid of what she might see. She opened it a crack. Instead of a deathly pallor, he wore a healthy flush. She had never seen him with so much color and life in his face. He looked at least ten years younger.

"Robert, I'm happy to see you looking so well," she said as

she entered the room. Then she halted in confusion. Timothy was standing by the bed, his expression unreadable. Had he told Robert of their love?

"My dear child, you don't know how happy you've made me," Robert said with pride shining in his eyes.

"Happy?"

"You aren't really my wife. That man was no minister." He got out of bed, fully dressed. "I'm not nearly as weak as I was pretending to be, and Timothy isn't merely my gardener. He's my heir."

"We're not married?" Mary asked, feeling as if her head was spinning.

"I'm sorry for the deception, but it was the only way I could be sure. I never married because I couldn't find anyone who suited me. I saw gold diggers everywhere, perhaps where none existed. I wanted to find someone worthy of Timothy so he wouldn't be alone like I've been. You, my dear, have proven to be a woman of morals, loyalty, and integrity. You'll make him a fine wife."

Mary had so many things to say that none of them would come out. She didn't know whether to be angry or to laugh in relief. She merely looked at Timothy in stunned silence.

"That is, if you'll have me," Timothy said quietly.

She quickly searched her heart. "Yes."

Timothy pulled her to him in a crushing embrace.

Robert chuckled. "The joke is on me. I thought I was settling a business arrangement. I never dreamed you would actually fall in love.

Cañon de Alegría

by Beth A. Maurer

◄━━✺

QUIETLY SHE WALKED to the cliff, as the sun began to warm the earth. The rosy hues of the sunrise blended with the majesty of the mountains   the earth and sky were one, just as they must have looked in the beginning of time, before God separated the expanses. This was her favorite time of day, a time to pause, a time to pray and give thanks, and a time to remember. She plaited the length of her silver hair, reflecting. Thirty years had come and gone—years of joy, years of sorrow. Like the soaring eagles, the moments flew over the mountains, back into her Canyon of Joy, dipping into her mind's sight, flowing away again, away on the roaring waters of the canyon river . . .

"There," she said, turning the key in the lock. "I've closed up for the last time." Tess Porter's smile was bittersweet. A life-

time of hard work and dedication had made the store success-
ful, but that was her parents' dream, not her own. The money
from the sale would allow her to pursue her own dreams, but
letting go of the past, all that had been her life, would not be
an easy transition. "No one ever said God's will was easy," she
muttered and turned the pages of time into a new chapter.

Her chestnut hair glistened in the sunlight, and her trim
figure often turned heads, but Tess was oblivious to this; her
mind usually focused on higher things. In less than a week, she
would be traveling into Mexico for the Christ World Mission
Network to work with an Indian tribe whose teacher had
retired. She would be responsible for the young children,
kindergarten to fifth grade. Fluent in Spanish, she was
relieved to learn that most of the Indians were bilingual, yet
she hoped to learn to speak and write the tribe's own language
as well.

Tess had packed carefully, but still it seemed that she had far
too much luggage. Try as they might, Wolf and Marta could
not fit it all into the jeep. "I am so sorry," she whispered as the
three stared, exasperated at the two remaining boxes that just
would not go. Two porters stood nearby, amused by their
plight.

"Señorita," one boy tried to hide his smile. "Perhaps if
you put the boxes in your seat and ride on the roof . . ." Both
porters bent double in peals of laughter.

Tess sighed, but her escorts brightened at the idea. Wolf
rummaged under the seats of the jeep until he came up with
several lengths of rope. Tess's eyes widened. "You're not going
to tie me on the roof are you?"

"Not you," the German missionary laughed. "That monster of a suitcase and your other bags. Then the boxes will fit in the jeep!"

Tess and Marta giggled together. The porter's joke had saved the day.

Tess stayed the first night with the young German couple. She discovered they both spoke a wealth of languages, including the language of the tribe she would be teaching. Wolfgang Chandler was the pastor of the small evangelical church in the village. There was also a Catholic church, the sanctuary of which would double as the school.

"Tomorrow, we will take you to your new home." Marta's permanent smile was warm and kind. "Rest well. We have a long day ahead of us!"

The road to the village was little more than two wheel tracks, which, were the jeep to veer to either side, would result either in serious damage from the nearly vertical rock face to the left, or a plunge of hundreds of feet on the right. Tess clung to the seat, praying that she would not be bounced out of the vehicle. For four hours she understood the verse "Pray without ceasing." Then, the car path stopped abruptly at the edge of a clearing. Climbing out of the jeep, Wolf "*hola*'d" loudly, and soon a man in faded jeans and a denim shirt, complete with cowboy hat and boots, appeared, leading several mules. "El alcalde," Wolf indicated—the mayor.

Tess nodded at the wizened little man. She could not begin to guess his age. He appeared ancient, yet he walked with the step of a young man.

"Señor Apate, el alcalde, will take you to the village," Wolf spoke in Spanish to Tess and the guide.

"You're not going along?" Tess felt a tiny stab of fear for the first time since she had signed on with Christ World Missions.

The alcalde pointed at her luggage. "Too many boxes, not enough mules. The preacher goes home, you come with me."

Her belongings loaded, Tess sat gingerly astride the little burro, moving into the unknown, listening to her connection to the outside world retreat back down the car path, not to be seen again for two whole weeks. Tess wondered if she would still be alive.

La aldea, the village, had no name, its people called themselves *Petapi*, after a great chief who had once ruled their tribe. The mule path led into the narrow village, first past the Catholic church-school that, Señor Apate informed her, also included the jail and *la tienda*, the store. Beyond the church rose several small houses, cabins really, hewn from what few large mesquite pines could be scrounged from the rocky mountainside. They stood dwarfed by the sheer rock face, towering high above the village, crude dollhouses in a giant's playroom, splashed with color from the few flowers that braved the altitude of Mexico's mountains. In the center of the village stood a block building that the alcalde informed her was the clinic. A doctor would visit once every three months. For emergencies, the village had to rely on a tiny field hospital, six hours down the canyon in the *Warapi* settlement.

Beyond the scattered cabins and the clinic, a well-weathered cabin bordered the edge of the precipice overlooking the canyon. Small but sturdy, the cabin would be the home of Tess

Porter for as long as she chose to stay. Were it not for the lack of transportation, she was sure she would have turned around that very minute.

Tess stared as a long line of people marched solemnly through the village. Someone beat a drum slowly, and the people sang in a doleful cadence. She felt strangely out of place when she saw the coffin they carried. She bowed her head reverently, but kept one eye trained on the procession. A young man walked behind the coffin, his face wreathed in sorrow and pain. He held the hand of a tiny girl who sucked her thumb, watching her papa with fearful eyes. "Wife and mother lost," Tess whispered. She prayed this sad day would not be an omen to her stay at the *Aldea de los Petapis*.

An axe rang out loud and clear at 6:00 A.M., echoing and reechoing down the canyon walls. Tess rose groggily from her bed, rubbing her eyes and groaning over her aching body. "If I never see another mule again . . ." she muttered to herself, then picked up her boot. As instructed, she turned it upside down and shook it, then banged it on the floor for good measure.

She didn't mean to scream, but once she let loose she couldn't stop.

"*Profesora!*" The voice came from outside. "*Profesora!* Are you okay?"

A young man hurried into the cabin. "*Profesora, està bien?*" The tiny scorpion on the floor and the new teacher standing on the bed screaming told him everything he needed to know. Grabbing the broom in the corner, he swept the creature out the door.

Returning, he asked, "Are you bitten?" Tess shook her head, suddenly embarrassed at her outlandish behavior, and equally embarrassed at the fact she was still in her nightgown. The man had bent down to retrieve her boots, and proceeded to pound them on the floor. His shoulders were shaking peculiarly, and Tess wondered if *he* was okay. "*Es todo.*" He smiled up at her. "That's all. I will return to your woodpile, now."

Only after he left did Tess realize he had been laughing at her. She allowed herself a giggle at her own expense, then set out to prepare for her first day in the village. After all, a teacher cannot teach in her nightgown.

"I forgot," Señor Apate stopped her. "Carlos de Pesaro will take care of your wood and carry your water."

Tess nodded ruefully, "We've met." She vaguely repeated her amusing story, sending the mayor on his way, chuckling. She was sure all would know of her scorpion encounter within the hour.

The church building was clean and neat. A small desk was provided for the teacher, and a chalkboard folded down from the ceiling against the wall at the front. She was surprised at the supplies available for the school, though slightly disappointed that she could not crusade to acquire needs. "Leave that to Christy Huddleston," she spoke to the empty room, and sat at the desk to compare her lesson plans with those the retired teacher had left behind.

The children wandered into the school before the sun had fully risen. Glancing at her watch, Tess discovered it was only seven o'clock. "You are early," she announced to the class, thinking to reward them for their promptness. The students' disappointed faces caused her some alarm. "No, no," she reassured them. "This is a good thing."

A thin girl in the front row, nearly in tears, burst out, "But papa said we were late!"

"Sí!" the boy next to her must have been her brother. "If we wait too long to come, the building is much too hot, and we cannot learn!"

Tess had not thought of this. Obviously air-conditioning was not a readily available commodity. Inwardly she groaned, realizing that she would have to start school at six-thirty, just to make sure all the lessons could be finished on time. Never an early riser, she knew that her woodcutter was to be her alarm clock from this day on.

The children were remarkably eager learners. Tess did not experience even one spark of trouble from her students. The parents, on the other hand, brought innumerable difficulties to her teaching day. They would stop by at any time, calling out to their children, asking how their day was going, asking if they were being good. With forty students in her class, divided between about twelve families, this meant at least two interruptions per hour in her five-hour class. Often these interruptions were only seconds, but one mother in particular gabbed with every child in the class, taking up nearly half an hour! Finally, in desperation, Tess asked the children, "Chanti, Rafael, what does your mother do especially well?"

"She cooks," Rafael answered hopefully, showing the clear way to his little man heart.

"She sews *el bordado*," Chanti answered proudly. "The best embroidery anywhere!"

"Would any of you like to learn this?" Tess asked her class.

Choruses of "Sí!" and bobbing heads confirmed the idea planted in Tess's mind. Why not begin classes of local interest, trade, and skill? Perhaps the interrupting parents could understand better how a classroom should operate if they could take part in teaching classes of their own!

Señor Apate was instrumental in helping her start the parent-taught classes. Within a week, her own classes were interrupted less, and the children enthusiastically reported learning to be more like their people, in the old ways and the new.

The semiweekly visits of Wolfgang and Marta were becoming a highlight to Tess. Not only did they bring newspapers and letters from her friends, they brought worship to the village. On Saturday evening, they would arrive and a great celebration would come to full swing.

Eagerly, Tess listened to the strains of music but little came to her understanding. She knew the English words to many of the hymns, but native songs of worship had no English relations and were lost on her untrained ears.

For weeks, she hummed the melodies of the choruses she could remember, standing at the precipice in the sunrise, praying for understanding to come to her heart.

"What are you singing?" Carlos de Pesaro stood behind her, listening to her feeble attempt at the words of the Indios. Tess turned to look at her woodcutter. She had not seen him smile since her encounter with Señor Escorpio. The sorrow that clouded his face never ceased to stab at Tess's gentle heart, for she had learned that it was the funeral of his wife she had seen the first day.

"It's a song about Jesus," Tess explained. "And it's about His love." She shrugged her shoulders. "But I don't know the words, because I don't know your language."

Carlos's shoulders sagged. "Not my language. The language of these people—they are my wife's people, not my own."

Tess tried to smile. "Then you are like me. A stranger in a strange land." Carlos stared off down the mountainside. "But you know the language—perhaps you can help me?"

Carlos shrugged noncommittally. He spoke something Tess could not quite hear.

"What did you say?" Tess tried to catch his gaze.

Carlos repeated the words. "It means 'This is God's sunrise.'"

He then turned and walked back to the woodpile. Tess repeated the phrase over and over, 'til she was sure she had it right. "Thank you, Jesus," she whispered, then hurried off to her children.

Carlos often stopped by her place of prayer to tell her new words and phrases. She tried to sound out the words of the songs to him, but he didn't know them either. "Perhaps if you came to the worship time," she tried to invite him.

"I believe in God," Carlos replied. "But I worship Him in my own way." He turned his sorrowful gaze upon her. "When I am angry, I chop more wood. My wife is gone; my child is motherless. I am angry. And I speak my anger to God with my axe."

Tess nodded. She understood the anger of grief. When the drunken driver had taken her parents' lives, she had been angry. The healing took time.

Excitement was high in the village. The Petapis were planning the great "Harvest Feast" when all the members of the village would gather to celebrate the bountiful harvest with music, dancing, and food. The children were restless at school, so Tess gave them a special assignment. They would write about the customs of the feast—the food, the native clothing, the dancing, and the singing. Especially important to Tess were the songs. She wanted the children to give her the words to the songs, first in their own language, and then with Spanish translation.

When the assignments were turned in, Tess hurried to her cabin, excited. Here, at last, was a small bridge to unity with her students and their people. Carefully, she read through the songs. "I can't wait to show these to Carlos," she announced to the goat foraging in her yard. She paused suddenly, blushing. "Now, why I am I blushing?" she asked the goat, then blushed still more. "Nonsense!" she muttered and stalked into the cabin, slamming the door behind her.

Carlos could sense her eagerness the next morning when she shoved the papers in his face. "Look what the children have done!" Her face was glowing with joy. Carlos watched her for a moment as she scanned the papers, choosing the first song she wanted to learn.

"What about this one?" she asked, pointing out a child's favorite ditty. Carlos sang the funny little song, then, looking at the student's translation, gave his approval. Carlos sat on a rock, Tess nearby, and for another fifteen minutes he sang songs and double-checked translations, giving both praise and corrections to the children's work.

Tess studied Carlos's face from the side. He was actually

smiling a little at the fun songs, and in the back of her mind, Tess allowed herself to admit that he was handsome. Descended from some great Spanish conquistador, splashed with the ruddy cheeks of the indigenous people, settled against the backdrop of the sunrise over the Mexican Grand Canyon, any woman's heart might have done a bit of acrobatics in his presence. Tess forced her own to still.

"Oh, my goodness!" Tess jumped up. "I'm going to be late! Adios! And *gracias*!"

Carlos watched her go, and his heart felt lighter than before. Whistling, he turned to chop her wood for the day.

Wolfgang and Marta arrived only a few hours after the celebration began, but since it was to last three days they weren't too disappointed.

"Enjoying yourself?" Marta smiled her trademark smile.

"This is so wonderful!" Tess's feet tapped to the rhythm as she watched the dancers whirl about to the native songs. "Occasionally, I even understand part of a song!"

"You're learning," Marta smiled. "Soon you'll be too much a part of them to ever want to leave."

Tess laughed with Marta, inwardly thinking she already had arrived at that point. She loved the people—loved her students. The view was grand, her cottage was cozy, and there was Carlos. "Now how did he get on that list," she thought, but smiled in spite of herself.

Carlos came to the celebration on the second day, dressed in the native costume of the Petapis, though he had regularly told Tess he was not one of them.

"Where have you been?" Tess smiled after he threaded his way to her, Rebecca in tow, thumb in her mouth. "I've been waiting for you to translate some of these new songs!"

Carlos looked happy to see her. He smiled often, now, and even laughed on occasion. "There are no new songs, here, *Profesora*." He gestured to the brightly clad people. "These are the songs of the ancients. They have been handed down for generations and will be echoing off the mountains for generations to come!"

"Perhaps you can teach me the new dance steps then," Tess spoke the words before she meant to, and quickly found herself among the people learning their native dance steps with Carlos as her *profesor*.

Later, Tess realized Carlos had not once left her side. She enjoyed his company. When Rebecca fell asleep in his arms, she was sorry to see him go. For her, the party was over, and she wandered home as well.

It was nearly midnight when someone pounded on her door. "*Profesora*!" Tess rose from her bed, alarmed. "*Profesora*!"

"Carlos?" Tess threw the door open. Carlos stood at the threshold, his hair wild, a lantern in his hands. "Carlos, what is it?"

"There is a puma prowling above the village." Carlos had been sent to spread the word. "*Profesora*, you must bar your door tonight, and your windows."

"There is no bar for the door." Frightened, Tess sought his gaze for comfort. "What shall I do?"

Carlos studied her for a moment. "The other villagers have been warned already. I will keep watch at your threshold. I will be the bar for your door."

Tess's clear blue eyes met his of deepest brown and found strength. She nodded her agreement, "*Gracias. Ten cuidado.*" Be careful.

Tess heard the puma scream once through the night. A shot rang out shortly after and then all was silent. The end of the cougar would be one more celebration to add to the third and final day of the feast. The harvest was in and all was well for another year. God was the Great Provider and the Protector of His people. And Tess's heart added her own thanksgiving for the protector at her threshold.

The last great day of feasting was loud and lively, yet by evening a hush descended on the crowd as the musicians announced the last song. Tess watched as couples rose to dance a slow, solemn dance in perfect step with each other.

"The children didn't write this song for me," Tess whispered to Carlos who held a sleeping Rebecca.

Carlos smiled over Rebecca's raven black curls. "This is not a song for children. "It is the '*Canta de Casa*,' the 'Song to Go Home To.'" Carlos watched the couples wistfully for a moment. Only last year, he had danced with his wife. He handed Rebecca to her "*abuelita*," and turned to Tess.

"*Profesora* . . . Tess, will you dance this last dance with me?" Hand in hand they joined the dancers where they danced to the song of commitment and devotion, the "Song to Go Home To."

Tess awoke with a start. The sun already shone in her window, but she had not heard the sound of Carlos's axe. Had she overslept? Had he not come to cut the wood? Hurriedly, she dressed and rushed to the school building, saying her prayers on the way. She was definitely late, for the children were already seated on the long hard benches, fidgeting as they waited for *la profesora*.

"Children, I am sorry I am late," Tess stammered. "The woodcutter did not wake me with his chopping this morning." The children laughed at her admission.

Pepito raised his hand.

"Sí, Pepito?"

"Señor Carlos de Pesaro received an urgent message of trouble in his village, *Profesora*," Pepito explained the man's absence. "He will not wake you for maybe many days."

"Oh, I see," Tess felt the color rise to her cheeks.

Pepito continued, "My brother and I can cut wood. Perhaps we can wake you!"

Tess smiled. "That would be most kind of you. Thank you, Pepito."

The rest of the morning dragged by as Tess's thoughts continuously turned to Carlos and their dance. How would she stand the next days without him if one morning should drag on for eternity? And what did the "*Canta de Casa*" mean to him? How long would she have to wait for the answers? And was this truly part of God's will for her? "God, please show me the way!"

Each morning, when the axe rang out, Tess dressed hurriedly to see if Carlos chopped her wood, only to greet Pepito and Alfonso. Each night, she stood at the threshold of her cabin and said to the night, "*Ten cuidado*." Daily she prayed for wisdom and strength, and in her heart, she sang "*Canta de Casa*."

Late one night, Tess heard shouting in the village. Hurrying to the door, she saw torches as an angry mob marched through the tiny community. "Where is the witch who teaches about Jesus?" She could hear their angry words echoing against the mountain. She realized their words were for her.

"*Profesora*," a little voice whispered. "They are the people of Carlos's tribe." A very frightened little Rafael slipped through the darkness. "They say you have poisoned his mind and ours!"

"Where is Carlos?" Tess hissed back at him.

"They say they killed him!" Rafael's whisper grew loud. "Bar your door, *Profesora*, and they will not get in!" With that, he melted into the darkness, and Tess was alone.

"Bar the door," she whispered. "God, I have no bar for the door, and Carlos cannot sleep on the threshold tonight." Tess fell to her knees and cried out, "God save me! . . . And tell Carlos I love him!"

The torchlight procession came into her yard and the light fell on the teacher, still on her knees.

"Pray to your Jesus, *Profesora*," one man jeered. "He cannot save you. He could not save Shanti and He did not save Carlos."

Tess found the speaker. Maldori, the brother of Shanti, Carlos's wife, blamed God and Carlos for her death. He had roused Carlos's village against Tess, calling her a witch with black magic called Jesus. Now, he wanted revenge against God with her as the sacrifice.

He approached, machete raised, as the crowd waited in silent anticipation. Tess watched his swing, as if in a slow-motion horror film. Another figure burst through the crowd, as Tess screamed.

"Carlos, no!"

"*Profesora!*" the call broke into her thoughts and memories. "You will be late, *Profesora!*" The laughing children hurried by on their way to school.

She flung her heavy braid over her shoulder and turned one last gaze to the eastern sky as the river flowed away, unstoppable in its path.

She glanced up at the silver-haired man, chopping the day's wood. He waved to her. She waved back and blew him a kiss.

"*Hasta luego*, Carlos," she called, and walked to the schoolhouse humming the "*Canta de Casa.*"

The Eyewitness

by James Shumaker

THEY WERE SUCH an unusual pair that they attracted stares from everyone who passed them on the streets of Rome. Here was a Roman, a citizen of the empire that surrounded the Mediterranean Sea, treating with familiarity a Jew, one of the conquered people. The citizen had a hand on the foreigner's back, while the Jew made gestures with his hands as he spoke. As the two rounded a corner, a woman stopped dead in her tracks because she could have sworn that the dominant Roman addressed the conquered Jew as "elder," a title of respect. Then, much to her disgust, she realized there went another citizen who had been infected with that new Jewish religion called Christianity.

Eventually, this odd couple came to the entrance of a house, and as they stepped up onto the porch, the Roman commented, "By now most of the people should be here for the meeting. They will be so excited when they learn that they have the privilege of meeting a newfound eyewitness."

At this, the Jew came to a halt and said, "Please, Rufus. Don't say anything about me being an eyewitness."

"But . . ." Rufus began to protest.

"Please, I have my reasons," he pleaded and looked the Roman intently in the eyes. Reluctantly, Rufus nodded his head in agreement.

The Roman pushed into the front door, and as he burst into the entrance hallway, Rufus shouted, "Claudia!" A woman in a white toga appeared at the opening of the hall. Her long brown hair was piled on top of her head and the two strands that hung past her temples were wet with perspiration.

"Rufus, am I glad to see you! I just handed out my last tray of fruit," Claudia said trying to catch her breath. Then she noticed the Jewish man. "Pardon my manners, sir. You must be Elder John. It is an honor to welcome you into our home." Claudia bowed slightly as she greeted her guest.

"The honor is all mine," replied Elder John as he returned the bow. "Your husband informs me that you host the largest gatherings of Christians in Rome."

The hostess looked slyly at Rufus and said, "We have a respectable crowd, but begging my husband's pardon, I would not be so bold as to say that it is the largest."

With that Elder John was escorted up the hall into a large room where the waiting audience formed a mixture of togas and Jewish robes. As John looked around the room, he saw about forty adults, along with a dozen or so children, seated on every rug and pillow that Claudia had available. The people seemed to be fairly relaxed as they talked and snacked from trays of fruit that the hostess had provided to them. All the conversations died down though when they noticed that Rufus had entered the room with his arm around a stranger.

"Dear friends and fellow Romans, I want you to meet Elder John," Rufus proclaimed. Excited murmuring filled the room as someone stated that the only Elder John they knew was a follower of Jesus. John rolled his eyes like *here we go again*, and Rufus quickly raised a hand to silence the audience. "No, no, brothers and sisters, the Apostle John is an older man. I met this John at the Apostle Paul's house. According to Paul, they first met fifteen years ago while he was staying at John's mother's house in Jerusalem. If I understood correctly, even the Apostle Peter was a regular visitor to their home."

Rufus continued the introduction by speaking for the next two minutes. The proud host repeated all the people and places that the elder had mentioned in their conversation on the way over to the meeting this evening. Although the details seemed very exciting and interesting to the crowd, it was obvious that the elder was becoming more and more uncomfortable as each new fact was mentioned. Rufus was almost finished when he began to say, ". . . and most importantly, he is . . ." The Roman stopped when he saw the panicked look in his guest's eyes. It was as if John knew what Rufus was going to say next. Deftly the host recovered and said, "He is going to do our reading tonight."

The crowd clapped in approval as Rufus motioned for Claudia to bring a scroll and give it to John. The ends of the parchment were curled around two wooden rods, so that it opened to approximately where the reading should begin. As the elder scanned the writing he exclaimed, "Oh, this scroll."

Embarrassed by his outburst, he immediately tried to explain his reaction. "I must apologize, brothers and sisters, but for some reason I feel very nervous tonight. I was expecting to read from the Law or the prophets, but instead you handed me *this scroll*." He shook the curled papers over his head with one hand. "I had no idea that you possessed one of the gospels of Jesus Christ. It is a rare privilege to be read to about the life and teachings of our Lord and Master." He then turned to Rufus who was standing behind him and asked, "Could you please show me where you are?"

Rufus pointed and said, "Right there, where it starts 'Then they came to a place.'"

John gave a questioning glance upward. Then after a deep breath, he was about to read when a knock was heard. Claudia dashed out of the room and soon the creaking of the front door opening echoed up the hallway. The crowd could not quite make out the conversation, but the tone of Claudia's voice seemed cautious and uncertain. Finally she led a man into the room and said, "Elder John, this man claims that he knows you."

Without giving John a chance to respond, the new visitor announced, "Sir, I was at the Apostle Paul's house at the same time that you were. You may not remember me, but I remember you. You are indeed the man that Paul proclaimed to be an eyewitness."

The color drained from Rufus's face as he became anxious about how the elder would react now that he had been exposed. Claudia covered her mouth in surprise since she was never let in on the secret, and the audience began to talk excitedly among themselves. Some were excited about the news while others were indignant that this fact was not made known to them from the outset. Even so, most people were honored to have an eyewitness as their guest reader. That is everyone except for one little boy in the front row. He leaned over to a friend next to him and said in a voice that carried throughout the whole room, "What's so great about being an eyewitness anyway?" The crowd gasped in dismay, but John looked at the boy with a good-natured grin and twinkle in his eye.

The guest of honor crouched down and used the scroll in his hand to motion the boy forward. He said, "Come up here, young man." The boy flushed red as he hesitantly approached the crouching elder. Once the boy was close enough, John put his free hand on the boy's shoulder and asked, "So what is your name?"

"Marcus," came the shy reply.

John laughed and rubbed the top of the lad's head. Then, looking straight into the boy's eyes, the elder said, "I should have guessed that you were a Marcus." He paused and looked around the room. The people were silently waiting to see what he would do next. Then he saw the remorseful look on Rufus's face. The host began to mutter an apology, but John stopped him and said, "No need to be sorry, my brother. I never should have kept my status as an eyewitness hidden."

The elder stood up and noticed that the gentleman who had exposed him was still at the hallway entrance and looking like he was poised to flee the room at any moment. The late-comer was not quite sure what he did, but judging from all of the conflicting emotions in the room, it must have been something wrong. Reassuringly, John spoke to him. "Come on in and have a seat. I was going to make a similar announcement myself before you even knocked at the door."

Again he knelt down to eye level with Marcus and put a hand on the boy's shoulder. "Finally, Marcus, nobody could have stated the main question for tonight any better than you." Then he addressed the audience, "What is so great about being an eyewitness?"

At this Claudia spoke up. "But Elder, it was just a childish, impertinent outburst."

"I disagree," replied John looking up at the hostess. "I think it is a very good question, and one that should have been approached a long time ago. Let me put it another way. Why is it when someone is lucky enough to see a major event in the life of Jesus, you call him an eyewitness and then heap more importance upon him than anybody else?"

The response was stunned silence, except for Marcus. Now he was impressed and exclaimed, "You saw Jesus?"

John meekly nodded his head and said, "Yes, I did." He paused and then continued. "Even so, my young friend, it makes me no more special than anyone else." Facing the crowd again, he asked, "How many of you here have experienced God's salvation?" Hands went up all over the room. "Then you too are Jesus' witnesses." Horrified that they had committed an act of blasphemy, several people quickly retracted their arms.

A sad expression came over the elder's face, then he noticed a pillow against the front wall. Assuming that it was reserved for the guest speaker, John slowly sat down on the cushion and pulled Marcus onto his lap. Then he said, "Brethren, when I looked into the scroll tonight the Lord spoke to me, and by your actions, you have confirmed that word." Taking a deep breath he added, "God has shown me that His church has turned to idolatry."

Several of the Jews made comments to the Romans in the crowd who had come from a notorious pagan tradition. In response, the accused complained that they had not entered a temple since they were saved. Finally the elder clarified his statement. "No, you are not guilty of worshiping statues of stone or wood or precious metals. No, your idols are made of flesh." He paused to let that thought sink in and then he continued, "The prophet Jeremiah once said 'Cursed is the man who trusts in man, and makes flesh his strength, whose heart departs from the Lord.' You ask how have you committed this sin, in that you rely so much on apostles and elders and, yes, even eyewitnesses, for your guidance that you have forgotten to seek God himself."

An eerie silence fell on the room, telling John that he had hit his mark. "Yes, God has set leaders over you to teach and instruct, but even so, we are merely fellow servants of Christ with you. We are flawed and need to pray to the Lord daily for our direction also." John looked to Rufus. "Brother, I love you with all of my heart, but unfortunately you are the most immediate example I have. When you introduced me tonight, I became nervous because you put me on pedestal where I did not belong. You exalted me as a man based on whom I knew and where I had been. That is not what I want people to know about me. No, my testimony is that I was in a wretched condition before I met Jesus Christ and that he has since changed me. The focus needs to be on Jesus Christ, not me.

"Now, concerning me being an eyewitness. The reason that I do not make it more publicly known is because it is a point of shame for me, not honor. Despite that, I knew as soon as I saw the text of tonight's reading that I was to share my eyewitness experience, because God wants you to understand the folly that the practice of assigning this title has become."

John picked up the scroll and stared intently at it. He seemed to be momentarily uncertain what to say next. Finally he said, "I was supposed to read to you the account of Jesus in the Garden of Gethsemane. My friends, I was at the Garden of Gethsemane the night that Jesus was arrested." Oohs and ahs emanated from the audience. John put up his hand and pleaded, "No, please, hold your adoration until after you have heard how I came to be in the garden that night.

"I was living in Jerusalem when the master, Jesus Christ of Nazareth, came to our city to spend the last week before his crucifixion . . ." As John began to tell his story, he was transported to another place and time in his mind. The large room of Rufus and Claudia's house became a very similar one that that was in his boyhood home. He and his mother lived back then in a two-storied mansion with a walled courtyard in front. Since John and his mother had such a large residence, it had become tradition for them to provide lodging for all of their out-of-town relatives during the holidays, especially Passover. John explained for the benefit of the Romans that Passover was an annual Jewish feast held in remembrance of the time several hundred years ago when God rescued his chosen people out of the land of Egypt. In fact, it was the week before Passover when Jesus of Nazareth arrived. Since it was also the time of purification in preparation for the feast, John and his mother already had a houseful.

By now the elder was so engrossed in his story that the

audience became his relatives. Besides the usual collection of aunts, uncles, and cousins, one person who stood out in John's memory was his grandfather. He was a very important man because he was one of the chief priests of the temple and a member of the Sanhedrin. Unfortunately he was not having a very good holiday this year. It seems that Jesus was a constant source of distraction from the normal holiday proceedings. As a result, the very mention of the wandering teacher's name would send grandfather into a rage.

Then there was Cousin Samuel who was two years older than John. For as long as he could recall, his older cousin was always the ringleader of some sort of mischief. This year, though, his activities had been restricted. Between Jesus leading a mob into the temple and then cruelly mistreating the merchants and bankers who conducted business in the outer court, grandfather was convinced that sooner or later there was going to be a riot. So for their own safety, all the women and all males under age eighteen were confined to the house.

All week, John had shared his bedroom with seven of his cousins, including Samuel. So when the day before Passover finally arrived, the boys had become pretty restless. That night, they were all up in John's room talking and wrestling around when they heard a knock at the front gate. Suddenly they all became very quiet and went to look out the second-story window of the bedroom so they could spy into the courtyard below. They watched as a servant-girl went to the gate and lifted the heavy wooden bar that kept it locked. As soon as she opened the door, several men with torches burst into the courtyard and asked to see grandfather.

Trying to be as quiet as possible, the boys watched as

grandfather and several other relatives went to talk to the men. As the men spoke, someone mentioned "Jesus of Nazareth." A couple of his cousins gasped, which caused an uncle to look over his shoulders. The little eavesdroppers immediately ducked down before they could be spotted. As they sat beneath the window's ledge, one boy whispered about how strange it was that grandfather did not get angry when someone spoke the forbidden name. John commented that he did not understand why everybody hated Jesus. He had heard that he had done several good deeds and performed miracles.

Just then there was the sound of shuffling feet outside. The little spies looked up in time to see grandfather and a couple of uncles leave with the mob. Immediately they speculated about where they could be going. Finally somebody suggested they were on their way to see Jesus. Then John dreamily stated that if that were true, he would pay money for the chance to go with them. By now the last man had finally exited, and Samuel noticed that the gate was left ajar. The older boy nudged John with his elbow and dared him to sneak out the half-open entranceway. John shook his head no, because he knew there was no way that his mother would even let him out of the house.

Then Samuel suggested that he go out the window. Well, John knew better than that. He would probably break his leg if he jumped from there. So the older boy began to explain how John could tie his coat and tunic together and use them as a rope to climb down the wall. Samuel would hold on to the top of it until he was safely on the ground. Shyly John took off his coat and was just about to pull his tunic over his head when he stopped and realized that he would be stripped down to his *sindon*, his linen undergarment. Samuel then got a strange smile on his face and promised to throw John's clothes down to him. With that assurance, he slipped off his tunic.

Once Samuel finished tying the two garments together, the other cousins stepped aside, leaving a clear path to the window. John walked slowly to the window and nervously took the makeshift rope into his hands. As he swung his right leg out the window and sat on the ledge, his toes tinkled. Seeing this hesitation, Samuel began taunting John. John looked over the courtyard wall and noticed the glow of torches had stopped just a few houses down the street. Knowing that they would soon be moving again, he took a deep breath and let himself fall out of the window. The rope jerked as John became suspended in midair. He hugged tightly what normally served as a coat and wrapped his knees around its dangling sleeve.

Just then Samuel encouraged him to hurry up because he could not hold John forever. So, slowly the frightened boy released his left hand and dropped it below his right. Then he pulled his legs apart, which allowed his body to slide a few inches. Actually, once he got started, climbing down the clothes rope was not that hard and he was amazed how quickly he found himself standing in the courtyard. As soon as John let go, though, the clothes rope was pulled back up into the window. He motioned for them to throw his clothes down. Instead Samuel just grinned mischievously at him and pointed off into the distance. John looked over his shoulder just in time to see the light from the torches disappear around a corner.

Realizing that he had to act quickly, John dashed across

the courtyard and out the half-open gate. As he ran to where he last saw the light, John felt the cold night air pass easily through his thin linen *sindon*, and his bare feet grew numb as they pounded the chilly cobblestones. Shivering, John was about to give up when something caught his eye. He saw torches go out of the gates of the city. Without thinking, he dashed toward the gate. Outside the city, he saw the men go around the corner of Jerusalem's extensive walls. He trotted to the edge and cautiously peeked around. The men were traveling up the road to the Mount of Olives.

With few obstacles to block his view and the darkness accenting the brightness of the torches, John was able to follow far enough behind the mob in order to avoid detection. Once the men entered the grove of olive trees, John quickly closed in. Now he could hide by darting from tree to tree. Eventually he was close enough to see that there were two groups of men. Several respected members of the Jewish community and a band of temple guards accompanied his grandfather. The other crowd was much smaller and seemed to be mostly poor workers.

John could not quite understand what they were saying, so he decided to creep closer. Before he could reach the next trunk, the two groups began shouting at each other. When John looked through the trees, he could see a large man in the robes of a fisherman swinging a sword in the midst of the crowd. Without warning, the fisherman lunged at a man, and John screamed in horror as he watched the victim's ear being cut off. He quickly ducked behind a tree and covered his mouth. *Hopefully nobody heard that*, he thought.

After a couple of minutes, the noise settled down and John

became brave enough to take another look. He saw one small group fleeing from the garden and another man with his hands tied together being led away by the temple guards. The young eyewitness was still trying to make sense of what he had just seen when suddenly a hand grasped his shoulder. He tried to break free, but the grip was too strong. Soon John felt more hands grabbing hold of him, and before he knew it, three young men had him completely restrained. One of them shouted, "Hey, I think we found a spy over here!"

John's heart leaped with fear as the mob turned in his direction. His grandfather and uncles were in that crowd. *What if they recognize him?* The thought made him feel even colder than he was before. Then John felt the hold on him loosen as his captors focused their attention on the approaching men. Realizing now was his opportunity, John ducked his head and put his arms straight out in front of him. With one fluid motion, he shed his *sindon* and started to run back toward the city. He was already disappearing amongst the olive trees when the young men noticed that they were clutching an empty linen cloth.

With his story coming to a close, John was once again aware that he was sitting on a pillow in front of an audience in a home in Rome. Marcus, who was still on his lap, asked, "So what happened next?"

"When I finally got home, the first person to see me was my mother. She was shocked to see me naked and half-freezing. She immediately ordered Rhoda to get a robe and a hot drink for me. While I sat being warm by the fire, I was forced to confess where I had been in front of everybody. Fortunately my grandfather did not get back until late the next morning, and by then I was sick in bed with a fever. Nobody told him about my little escapade. I guess my mother figured that getting sick from being in the night air and improperly dressed was punishment enough."

Elder John then addressed the audience directly, "Which brings me to the question asked earlier: What is so great about being an eyewitness? Fortunately most of the people who you call eyewitnesses are God-fearing men." John again picked up the scroll, "Take the author of the scroll that you have been reading, the Apostle Peter. Here is a man who is truly worthy to be honored as an eyewitness, because he was more than a spectator watching an event. He walked with Jesus for three years and that is why you can trust the scroll that he has written."

Someone in the audience stood up and interrupted, "But elder, in the introduction of the scroll that you are holding, it says that the gospel was not written by Peter, but by . . ."

John stopped the speaker by putting up his hand and then explained, "Yes, it states that it was written by somebody else. But don't forget that it starts off with *The Testimony of Simon Peter.*" A pained look came over the elder's face. Then he continued, "I have even heard rumors that this particular scroll is being named after the writer, which is regrettable. Just because Peter was illiterate does not make him any less the author. Everything in this scroll is his words and his story, except for a couple of lines that the writer added in himself. Even so, I think if you were to ask the writer, he would have gladly left off his name completely, rather than have it take precedence over Peter's name.

"But we are getting away from the subject. My point is

that the original idea of eyewitnesses was not a bad one, but it seems that lately the church has been lowering its standards. If the criteria for being an eyewitness is a disobedient thirteen-year-old boy who just so happened to be in the garden the night that Jesus was arrested, then anyone who crossed the Lord's path while he walked this earth is worthy of this title."

The elder paused for a few seconds. Then he continued, "When I talk to the leaders of the church, one of their great fears in that a wolf will come in sheep's clothing and destroy the flock from within. Not everybody with a tale to tell can be trusted. I am concerned that somebody with an eyewitness account to tell could possibly infiltrate a body of a believer, and based on his story alone, take control of that body and lead it astray. Don't trust people just because they come with title of pastor or apostle or even eyewitness. Pray to God for discernment so that you will not be deceived."

Before the guest speaker could say another word, somebody started pounding on the front door. Once again Claudia dutifully went to answer. After a brief conversation, she shouted, "Elder John, could you come here please?"

John gently slid Marcus off of his lap and onto the pillow. Then he got up and disappeared into the hallway. After another short exchange, the elder came back into the room. "I am sorry, folks, but something has come up which requires my attention." Looking at Rufus, he said, "Maybe I can come back another time and read the scroll for your group."

"I would like that very much," replied the host.

"Well then, I will see you later," said John, but before he could leave the room everyone in the audience simultaneously stood up and lunged toward the elder. They all wanted to personally wish him goodbye and say how they were touched by his teaching.

While most people's backs were turned to him, Marcus reached for the scroll and began to unroll it. "See anything interesting?" a deep voice asked and the boy looked up into Rufus's face. Fear and guilt filled the child's expression, but when Rufus smiled kindly at him, the child relaxed.

"I cannot read it," confessed Marcus. "It has all these funny symbols. It is not Latin."

"No," said the kind man. "This is Greek."

"Can you read it?" questioned the boy and Rufus nodded his head affirmatively.

Taking the role of a teacher, Rufus stated how this was the text that Elder John was going to read tonight. He was interpreting the foreign characters for Marcus when a phrase caught his eye. It translated, "And the young men laid hold of him, and he left the linen *sindon* and fled from them naked." Rufus threw a glance toward his guest still being thronged and mumbled softly, "No, it couldn't be."

As he leaped to the beginning of the scroll, Rufus could hear John saying to someone, "Yes, I am always being mistaken for the Apostle John. When I was a boy I went by my surname; I am thinking about using it again in order to eliminate that confusion." Finally Rufus reached the introduction, which read, "The Testimony of Simon Peter As Written by John Mark."

Eagles' Wings

by Cindy Kane

ANGIE SIGHED AND slowly straightened up. She pushed her damp hair back from her eyes with a shaking hand and looked at the porch to see if Grant was awake and needing her. A glance told her that she still had a little while longer to get the weeds pulled.

A gliding shadow caused her to look up. There flying slowly above was the same large eagle that she had noticed every day this summer. It never made any sound, just circled a few times and silently moved on to the mountain in the distance. Angie loved to watch it. It soared so effortlessly on the wind, a freedom to its flight that pulled at her heart.

She shook her head and tried to focus back on the task before her. If she didn't hurry she would have to leave the job half done and finish it tomorrow when Grant had his nap. She bent over again and for the next hour took her buried frustrations out on the weeds.

Later that night Angie settled into the old high-back rocking chair by the window and looked out at the distant mountain. In the evening light it took on a peaceful look. Its craggy peaks were dressed in purple and pink hues as the sun settled low on the horizon, as if awaiting a signal to end the day. Angie drew her knees up and wrapped her arms around them while drinking in the scene before her. The wild roses out by the pasture fence lent their scent to the evening breeze as it moved its way to stir the old lace curtains in the windows. Angie breathed deeply the fragrance that came to her on the cooling breeze. She relished this time to herself at the close of the day.

Before Grant had suffered the stroke, they used to sit on the porch and watch their mountain change color in the twilight. No two evenings were ever the same. Some nights the mountain burned a fiery red and orange, other nights were tranquil with muted pinks and violets. They used to sit shoulder to shoulder and try to guess what the mountain would decide to wear each evening. They made a game of it with the loser making breakfast the next morning. Those were happy and carefree days; even though they struggled to keep up the payments on the ranch, they were content living in the shadow of the mountain.

Trembling, Angie drew her knees tighter to her body as memories drew her back to that frightening day last fall when Grant hadn't come home. She had paced the front porch watching the main road for the old green truck that never arrived. Instead a neighbor had turned into the gated drive that led to the old ranch house. Grant had suffered a stroke at the "Feed & Seed" in town; did she need a drive to the hospital? The next months were a heart-wrenching blur; life as she had known it disappeared forever.

After two months in the hospital and four more spent in rehab, Grant came home. Gone was the strong, dashing dreamer who had cared for her with a ravishing love that took her breath away. In his place was a broken spirit confined to a wheelchair. He couldn't even speak plain enough to make his simplest requests known. Angie died a little each time she looked into those dark eyes that now held such hurt and confusion. Sometimes Grant welcomed her help, but other times the smoldering anger directed at her made her shake. She knew he envied her ability to do what she wanted without help. It wasn't her fault she would silently scream back at him. Did he think she enjoyed caring for someone who resented her? Or that she liked trying to run a ranch that was going bankrupt? Did he think she liked trying to keep a house looking nice when there was no money for all the repairs that needed to be done? Angie shivered, more at the unfairness of it all than from the cold breeze that was now blowing in at the open window.

Sugar the cat tried to jump up and Angie put her legs down to accommodate the demand. "All things work together for good" (Romans 8:28 KJV) came unbidden to her mind. Sure, she bitterly thought. Everything her grandmother had taught her about God seemed too distant now. What kind of God would let this happen, she asked herself for the hundredth time. But she stopped; the next part of the verse said, "To them that love God," and she wasn't on speaking terms with Him anymore. The last time she had prayed had been at

Grant's bedside that fateful night. "Lord, give me back my husband," had become a mantra to her as it was repeated over and over. But no, God had not given her back her husband. He had given her back a stranger and in the process ruined her life. No, she thought, she didn't want any kind of relationship with a God like that.

Angie stood up abruptly, dumping a protesting cat onto the floor, and went to make sure the doors were locked. She then made her way to the spare bedroom where she had been sleeping since Grant had come home. It was time to end this day, although tomorrow held no promise for her.

Angie was hanging out the laundry the next morning when the sound of a car coming up the drive made her turn. Shading her eyes against the brightness of the morning sun, she tried to figure out who was approaching. As the car rolled to a stop in front of the house Angie suppressed a groan. Squaring her shoulders and trying to put on a convincing smile, she went forward to greet Emma Stevens, the pastor's wife from town.

In the months since Grant's stroke, every effort by the Stevenses to reach out to this young couple had been rebuffed, and yet they kept coming, always pleasant. To Angie it seemed that nothing short of screaming at them to leave her alone would make them stop visiting. There was nothing she could do except smile and thank them politely for their prayers. Emma came toward Angie with a smile and a whispered prayer that God would direct her words to this hurting heart.

Angie sat on the porch steps, her laundry forgotten in the basket, and stared at the departing car. Her head was still spinning with the possibility of the offer just proposed. Did she dare? The offer seemed too good to be true, and yet she had heard it with her own ears . . . could she? How could she not? The thought of accepting made her breathless!

"So how did it go today, honey?" asked Brad Stevens as he reached for another helping of his wife's potato salad.

Emma looked across the table at her husband and smiled.

"I think she might do it, although she was shocked speechless at the offer."

Brad chuckled as he savored the mouthful of fried chicken he had just taken. He could well imagine the look on Angie Miller's face when she heard the plan. Prayer opens the door for miracles, he thought, and Angie was due for one.

Angie settled into bed with a sigh. Today had been an especially hard one with Grant. No matter what she had done for him, it had been met with stubborn resistance. She punched the pillow into a comfortable shape and curled onto her side so she could see out the window. The mountain was bathed in light from the full moon. It had a mysterious aura about it as shadows danced just beyond the reach of the moonbeam fingers.

Angie soaked in the peaceful picture as her mind turned to the invitation extended yesterday by Emma. She quivered with excitement as the thought of three days away from the ranch presented itself again. She wondered why Pastor Stevens would want to move in and care for Grant; it wouldn't exactly be a vacation for him. The only drawback that she could see was the condition that came with the offer. He would come and care for Grant so that she could be Emma's guest at a Ladies Retreat held at Camp Freedom, located at the foot of the mountain. Angie wasn't interested in attending the Retreat, but how welcome a three-day break would be. She had promised to let Emma know by tomorrow if she was interested in their proposal. After the day she had just gone through, the decision was an easy one. She would call the Stevenses in the morning and accept their offer. She looked at her mountain again. In four days' time she would be at the base, and she quivered again in excitement.

Angie glanced back at the house and marveled that she was actually on her way. The last few days had been filled with doubts and second thoughts. But the promise of a few days of freedom had propelled her plans forward. She shrank from the memory of alarm that had come to Grant's eyes this morning when he had learned of her departure. The calm assurances of the Stevenses had done little to alleviate the guilt that had flooded her being.

Angie turned as she realized that the petite woman beside her had asked a question. She fumbled frantically in her mind trying to remember her name. It had been mentioned when they were introduced, but she had still been rattled by the look Grant had given her when she left.

"I'm sorry, I didn't mean to startle you," the young woman timidly apologized.

"That's okay," Angie answered, "I was just daydreaming. What did you ask?"

"I was just wondering if you had ever been to one of these Retreats before?"

"No," Angie said, and I wouldn't be now if I wasn't so frantic to get away for awhile, she finished silently. She turned back to the window, shutting off any further conversation. She wasn't trying to be unfriendly, but she needed to get her emotions under control.

She listened dispassionately to fragments of conversation around her during the next two hours. The church van in which they were traveling held six women from the area. Angie recognized everyone but her seatmate from the small church in town. Emma Stevens was driving, and occupying the other front seat was Margaret Thomas, the church librarian. The middle seat held Pearl Douglas and Ruth Conrad, both older women with grown families. They chatted about their grandchildren who were scattered around the country. Occasionally they turned and addressed the two younger women in the rear seat. Angie was content to let the young woman by her side respond to their queries. In so doing she learned that her name was Leah Bentley, and she was new to the area.

Glancing out the window Angie was surprised to see her eagle surfing the wind. Her nerves seemed to settle as this familiar presence continued to swoop overhead.

Camp Freedom had been in existence for nearly forty years and had just recently undergone a facelift. Ten new cabins had been built in a semicircle around the camp chapel. Much to Angie's relief, brand-new washroom facilities had replaced ancient outhouses.

As she moved her belongings into her assigned cabin, she noticed that her seatmate from the van was going to be her bunkmate. They smiled at each other as they spread out their sleeping bags on the paper-thin mattresses. As two other ladies came in loaded down with sleeping bags and suitcases, Angie slipped out the door. Leaving the laughter behind, she decided to use the free time before lunch to explore the camp.

Camp Freedom was nestled right against the base of the mountain that rose majestically behind the chapel. She noted over the chapel door a large wooden sign with a verse burned into the wood. "I will lift up mine eyes unto the hills, from whence cometh my help" (Psalm 121:1 KJV). To the right of the chapel was a large bonfire pit surrounded by logs used as seats. Near the driveway was the main office with a large playground to the left; and to the right she saw a new dining room that could seat a hundred hungry campers. A bubbling brook wound its way cheerfully through the camp. Angie found herself excited at the thought of three days spent in this lovely setting. She was glad she had come.

After a feast of homemade subs and scrumptious desserts, the ladies crowded into the rustic wooden chapel for the first meeting. Angie looked regretfully out the window as she chose a seat at the back. She wished she could sneak out and go for a walk through the inviting woods. But this was payment time for the weekend away, and she wasn't going to break her word, although in such a large crowd she was sure Emma wouldn't see her leave.

Later as she thought about the meeting, she wasn't sure just when her attention was caught. She had to admit that she enjoyed the singing. It was upbeat and created an atmosphere of joy that, though not personal, did surround her.

Then someone asked, "Has your heart been broken, your spirit weighed down with burdens too heavy for you to carry? Does your future look dismal with no hope, no escape?"

Tears had formed pools in Angie's eyes as she found herself silently answering yes to all the questions.

"Then lift up your eyes, for the Lord says that 'He is nigh unto them that are of a broken heart'" (Psalm 34: KJV).

No, Angie had silently argued, the Lord has deserted me; I'm alone with my burdens. She slipped out the chapel door and escaped to the woods that had earlier beckoned to her.

Angie walked for nearly twenty minutes before she found a path that seemed to start up the mountain. There was no hesitation as she turned and started up the steep incline. The beauty around her seemed to quiet the inner turmoil as she climbed higher and higher during the next hour. Finally needing to catch her breath, she found a seat on a rock and sank gratefully down. Slipping off her shoes she wished for a cool brook in which to soak her aching feet. She settled instead for giving them a good rub as she gazed out over the valley below. Turning her gaze upward, something caught her eye. It was her eagle! Angie watched this acrobatic wonder until it disappeared into a crevice somewhere high overhead.

Part of a verse she had memorized as a child came to her mind, "They shall mount up with wings as eagles." Funny, she thought, that after all these years this would come to her. She couldn't remember the rest of the verse, so who "they" were escaped her. But she found herself envious of whomever they were, being able to fly like an eagle above the drudgery of life.

Angie made her way back to camp just in time for supper. She was glad because her hike had worked up quite a hunger. The lasagna and salads did wonders in satisfying the empty hole in her middle.

After supper there was an hour before the evening service. Angie made use of the time to shower and freshen up. She was surprised that she didn't feel tired after her strenuous work-out. Instead, the fresh air had given her rosy cheeks and a sparkle to her eyes that had been missing for months.

Emma noticed the change in Angie's face as they made their way together toward the bonfire pit where the praise time was going to take place. She had been praying ever since she had seen Angie slip out of the afternoon service that God would bring His healing touch to this young woman's heart.

The fire was already ablaze as the women settled on the logs scattered around the area. The setting sun was coloring the mountain pink above them, and the gurgling brook was already singing.

Angie found herself clapping along with the rousing cho-rus, falling once again under the delightful spell of the gath-ering. During testimony time someone quoted a verse, "From the end of the earth will I cry unto Thee. When my heart is overwhelmed: lead me to the rock that is higher than I" (Psalm 61:2 KJV). Angie's attention was once again captured.

Angie tossed on her bunk that night, unable to sleep. She knew if she didn't stop she would soon be disturbing the oth-ers. She slipped quietly out of her bunk, put on her sweater, and, picking up her shoes, crept silently out the door. She made her way to the bonfire pit and sat down. The fire had been out for hours, but the air still held the tangy smell that she liked. The brook babbled softly to itself, as if afraid it might disturb the sleeping campers. Moonlight played with the side of the mountain as Angie settled herself on the ground in front of one of the logs.

She thought again about the verse the speaker had closed the evening with, "But they that wait upon the Lord shall renew their strength: they shall mount up with wings as eagles, they shall run, and not be weary; and they shall walk and not faint" (Isaiah 40:31 KJV). She had been shocked to hear the verse of her afternoon musings. Her question as to who the "they" were had been answered. The "they" were those who waited upon the Lord . . . and she didn't qualify.

Angie felt her eyes fill with tears. She was tired of struggling alone with the burdens of life. She wanted her strength renewed, she wanted to mount up with eagles' wings. She wanted to soar with the promises of God. It was her fault that she was weary and faint. She had stopped waiting on the Lord; she had tried to do things on her own and then had blamed God when everything fell apart around her.

She bowed her head and cried. She wept for the long months lost in self-pity, wept for Grant and their marriage, wept in repentance of her bitterness. But mostly she cried out her need to have her strength renewed by her loving Heavenly Father who had been waiting to heal her broken spirit.

As peace gradually penetrated her tired body, she looked up and realized that dawn was approaching. A verse her grandmother used to recite echoed in her mind, causing her to smile. "Weeping may endure for a night, but joy cometh in the morning" (Psalm 30:5 KJV). Yes, there were still problems, there would still be days ahead of hardship with Grant, but morning joy had come at last. She still did not know why things had happened as they had, but she was once again on speaking terms with the One who did know, and she felt contentment come with this knowledge.

A step sounded softly behind her. Standing in the predawn light was Emma. She noted the peace on Angie's face and knew her prayers had been answered. As they moved into each other's arms, high above the eagle soared into the promise of a new day.

The Lint-Lender

by Donna Burton

~⌒⌐

For pete's sake, Mama. What in the world are you saving
these things for?" My tone well-defined the dismay I felt at
discovering yet another stash of plastic tubs tucked under the
already bursting pantry shelves. Jim and I were staying with
Mama and Daddy for a few weeks while Jim worked in the
office of a local client designing an ad campaign. This was a
great opportunity for Jim to obtain a long-term contract for
this client. Our decision that I take some time off to travel
with him and build his client base gave us the flexibility to visit
for a while. Jim felt right at home at my parents' and had come
to love them as he would his own. It was not hard being home,
just hard to move around in some areas of the house. We have
been married two years and have yet to stay in one place
longer than six months, so I have become accustomed to living sparsely. I love my parents, but the perpetual clutter of

"usable" items in their house has always bothered me.

"Oh, those are great for sending food over to old Mrs. Fisher. She can only eat a small amount at one time ya know. Since the old man died she has lost so much weight. Yer Daddy and I take over some of those containers once a week or so. Just little bits of things I cook."

"Mother, doesn't Mrs. Fisher live in the in-law suite Cindi built on to the house after her mother gave it to her and Ronnie? Can't Cindi cook for her mother? Why do you have to do it and clutter up the house even more with these stupid margarine containers? Everyone else throws them away, but you have to save them and everything else that 'might' be used one day. Don't you get tired of the clutter?"

"Oh, Dana, you know that yer Daddy and I always try to make good use of things. We don't have to cook for old Mrs. Fisher. We want to do it. Cindi works full-time since Ronnie left her for that Stripling lady, and she doesn't have much time to cook. Those two children of hers keep her busy and she mostly picks fast-type food. The old lady just doesn't like that kind of food too much, so we take her some home-cooked bits now and then. It's no trouble for us to put a dab of this and that in those little tubs and carry it on over to her. No trouble at all." Her blue gray eyes, like the sky before a storm, softened as she continued, "She comes to the door and asks us in when we take the little tubs over. She always has the ones from the week before washed and ready for us. Most times she adds one or two more than what we brought. We sit with her a bit and she talks a little. Age is really settlin' in or her, ya know."

"Mama, how old is she anyway? I bet she is only a few years older than you and Daddy. She talks? About what? She never talked to you or anyone else that I know of." Mrs. Fisher, along with her husband, her snooty daughter Cindi, and her son had lived down the road from Mama and Daddy as long as I can remember. They had never been known in this small farm and "divided lot" community as kind, hospitable, or even nice neighbors. During my eighteen-plus years of living down the road from them, I never remember a single positive thing coming from that frame house with the concrete driveway. My brothers and I would joke about the concrete drive pulling out on a dirty and gravel road. Why they moved out here to begin with was a mystery. I never knew of them participating in any community or church events. Cindi was so stuck-up in school that no one seemed to be close to her. When she married Ronnie Centos we were all shocked, until eight months later when we learned of little Ronnie's arrival. No one ever said anything though. You just didn't here. I had left home five years ago to go to school and married after graduating. I had not really been home except to visit since I left, but the thought of such a change in Mrs. Fisher from the woman I knew was hard to believe. "Seems to me that getting old would only make her meaner," I continued.

Cindi Fisher was the kind of girl who made fun of the poor kids as they got on the bus. She was the girl who had the clothes, the hair, etc., but always wore a scowl toward everyone else. Sid, her older brother, was as close to a thug as anyone could be as a student at a small rural county high school. Mr. Fisher was loud, smoked stinky cigars, and loved to stop by to complain to my father about our dog Ajax getting into his trash. Ajax was a border collie and my six brothers had trained him well. He spent most of his time on our front porch, waiting for one of us to play or throw a stick. He was not a trash digger, but he was always blamed for the mess on the Fishers's front lawn. Daddy would always listen for a while and then ask if Mr. Fisher had seen Ajax in the trash. "Seen him? I don't need to see him," he would bellow. "I know it was him. You don't need to see an animal doing something to know he did it. In my business you learn to read people, Heiger. You read people and make the sale, that's what I always say." Puffing his stinky cigar he could go on for an hour on the fine points of selling, bragging about stealing this client or getting the customer to pay more than they should have. I was never exactly clear about what he sold, some type of plumbing fixtures, I think. Daddy listened and occasionally offered an unheard comment. "Oh well, I guess I better be heading up the hill, eh Heiger?" A slap on Daddy's shoulder and a "Try to control that dog of yours will you, Heiger" signaled the end of yet another house call by the greatest of all living sales reps.

Mrs. Fisher was kind of like a hawk with a cigarette hanging out of its mouth. I never heard her yell and could count the number of times I actually heard her say anything; she rarely even answered if you asked a question. My brothers and I would fight over who would have to go to her door to deliver mail or a package left at our house by mistake. Mother was forever having us "run somethin'" over there, like a pie or some other neighborly homemade item. We hated looking at her with her clouds of smoke being the only indication that she was even breathing.

"Mostly she talks about Sid," said Mama. "She talks about

him when he was little. How he picked flowers for her and ran to her with them and things he said when she brought Cindi home. Things like that mostly."

"Does she ever say thank you?" I asked.

"No, not in so many words. Yer Daddy and I know she 'preciates it though," Mama sighed.

"How do you know that, Mama? She never appreciated anything else you ever did. Pies, bread, homemade jelly, flowers in pots, or any of the other things you asked the guys and me to haul up there for years. As long as I can remember. Did she ever even once say thank you? Not that I heard, she didn't."

"Me and yer Daddy know she 'preciates it, Dana, that's all. We just know. The Fishers and us, we have history."

"You are forever doing something for somebody like the Fishers, Mama. You always have and it worries me that you are wearing yourself out doing so much. Our house has always been cluttered with plants you grow to give away or clean canning jars returned from someone to whom you gave apple butter. Fabric scraps from expensive dresses that fat Mrs. Gainer had the seamstress make for her by the bag. What in the world made her think you wanted those, Mama?"

"You know why, Dana. It's the quilts. Mrs. Gainer sends me the scraps for the quilts," she almost whispered.

"Mother, you haven't needed to make a baby burial quilt in thirty years or more. We have drugs to fight that now and you know you will probably never need to make another one. Tell Mrs. Gainer that you don't make those quilts anymore. Let her do what everyone else with a fifty-dollar-a-dress dressmaker does, and leave the scraps behind. Stop letting these people clutter the house. It's not like these are Christian people, Mama. That 'Mrs.' Gainer has supposedly been 'married' to five or six men and everyone knows she uses them for as much as she can get out of them."

Hearing the clothes dryer beep, I moved to the laundry room. "Just tell these people, Mama, that you are retiring, that's all." Opening the small utility cabinet to find a dryer sheet, I noticed a large plastic bag filled with a strange-looking grayish fluff.

"What's this, Mama?" Answering my own question, my nose crinkled as I pulled up a handful of dryer lint from the already overly full bag.

"Are you saving *this* now, Mama?"

Looking closely at the bag as if she was unsure of what I was referring to, Mama slowly shook her head. "Why, yes, Dana. I am saving that."

Breathing deeply, I posed the question. "Alright, since I cannot imagine what in the world you could possibly be saving laundry lint for, please tell me."

"Oh, Dana. It's not a big thing, just a bag of lint. For old Mr. Watkins, you know. Yer Daddy and I ran into him a few weeks ago at the store. Has to use a walker now to get around. Talked to us in the pickle aisle for almost thirty minutes. He asked about you. Still calls you his 'best girl ever.' Says he never sold anything before or since like he sold when you worked there. He was walking around that Super Wal-Mart like he was still checking out the competition, even though he closed his store years ago. His wife died and ya know he never had any children."

"Mother, what could that old skinflint possibly need laundry lint for? He must be a millionaire several times over. Before that Wal-Mart opened, his was the only store for twenty miles that carried anything except beer and cigarettes. Besides giving me a job, the same as he did for lots of other kids, and paying me almost nothing for working like a slave, what did he ever do for you?"

"Oh, Dana. Old Mr. Watkins was good to yer Daddy and me over the years. You know that havin' eight children was not always easy on the old wallet. Sometimes cash money for shoes and things like that was a bit hard to come by. Once they got bigger, old Mr. Watkins would always let yer Daddy and brothers do little jobs around the store. Things like repairing the roof, or fixing a hinge on one of the display cases, that kind of thing. Yer Daddy would take his pay in shoes or dress goods or whatever we needed at the time. It all worked out. God always provided a way for us, usually right quick after yer Daddy and me would pray about it too."

"I know all about Mr. Watkins's 'generosity,' Mama. I lived here too, remember. I remember going down there to try on shoes and sometimes he gave us candy. But that still does not answer my question, Mama. What about the lint?" Turning out the light and guiding Mama down the hall back to the cozily cluttered kitchen, I continued to push for an answer.

Chuckling, Mama replied, "Oh, Dana girl, you just don't see it yet. You are young and just startin' out with your real livin'. Some of us older folk have put through some things that make us feel in our heart what to do. God gave me and yer Daddy all of you children and each other and we are grateful to Him for how good he has been to us all these years.

Things are just here to be used, so me 'n' yer Daddy use them."

Putting an arm around her waist, I hugged her close and brushed the now all-gray bangs out of the way to plant a kiss on her crinkled forehead. "I'm sorry, Mama. I know you help out people with what you have on hand. I didn't mean to make you feel bad or bring up sad memories. I shouldn't have said that about the quilts. I know it was very hard for you, hard on Mrs. Gainer too. You know that, right? Do you "give me'?"

"Oh, Dana girl, nothing to ask forgiveness for. I'm yer Mama. I love you no matter how smarty mouth you are. Nothin' wrong with askin' questions. Best way to learn, I always say. Let's make some pound cake for supper. You remember the double butter one, don't you? We will triple the recipe and send one with Jim to that office. Nothin' like a good pound cake to seal the deal."

"Who told you that one—Mr. Fisher?" I bellowed, and retrieved my long-unused imitation of his stance and gait from the archives of my numerous impersonations.

Mama laughed until tears formed in her eyes, while scolding me for speaking ill of the dead. "You are a mess, girl. You know that. Me 'n' yer Daddy and brothers never needed much outside entertainment with you around, that's for sure."

Laughing, I reminded her that she had still not told me about the lint.

"Oh, Dana, that lint is for Mr. Watkins to put around his house for the birds. If birds have it available, they will use it for their nests and build them real close to where they can get the nesting materials. He told yer Daddy that he just loves to watch and feed the birds around his house. Every day he puts out seed and bread for them. Never had time to watch them when he was running the store, I guess. He needs those birds and the lint helps them to want to stay around."

Jim got the client. Our visit ended weeks later and we settled just six hours away. Other jobs, a house, and children have come along in the almost twenty years since that conversation. The drive required to visit gives me quiet time to think. Mama and Daddy's is just Daddy's now. Mama is over in Lawnwood between baby Dena and the place for Daddy to once again lie beside her. Flowers are planted all around their site, and even in winter color is supplied by the plants.

The house is still cluttered. I long to see plants growing in those pots or smell food cooking to be divided into dabs. Being the only surviving girl, I know that when the time comes the job of cleaning out the house will fall to me. My daughters will help Jim and me, and the boys will do what we ask. My brothers will be here, but will be of little use in deciding what to do with all of this stuff. I will do what I need to do.

Pulling into the Wal-Mart for supplies, I thought I recognized a woman crossing the parking lot. Oh well, probably not anyone I know.

My sisters-in-law rotate having Daddy over, but I know he likes to eat at home when I am there. While I'm pushing a cart through the store, I almost run into Cindi Fisher and realize she was the woman I earlier thought I knew crossing the parking lot. I never did call her Cindi Centos.

"Hey, Dana?" she queried.

"Why, hello Cindi. I thought that was you. How are you?"

"Okay, I guess. Are you visiting your Daddy?"

"Yes, I try to come up once a month or so. Sometimes I just can't make it every single month, though. How are your kids?"

"Well, little Ronnie is still in the air force and Sara is a teacher at the elementary school in Harpsburg. Both of them are married, but no grandchildren yet. I retired on disability from the telephone company a year ago, and live by myself in that big house."

"Retired? Cindi, it's hard to believe that we are getting old enough to retire. I still remember you getting on the school bus wearing those pink pants."

"You remember the pink pants? My goodness, I haven't thought about those things in years." She smiled only for a dab of a second.

"Dana, I was at yer Mama's service. I know you probably didn't know I was there because there were so many people that I couldn't get close enough to see you."

"That's okay, Cindi. I understand."

"After Sid killed himself, yer Mama and Daddy came almost every day to bring us something. After Daddy died, yer Mama and Daddy came by once a week with those sweet little tubs of food for my mother. Yer mama was the only friend I ever remember coming into our house to see my mother. I never thanked her."

Moving around the cart, I put my hand on her shoulder. "It's okay, Cindi. Your mother and Mama understood. They had history, you know, and they understood. Don't worry about it, okay? Anyway, what are you doing with yourself now that you are a retired lady?"

"Well, I take care of the house and the yard and that sort

of thing. I go over to Lawnwood once a week with flowers. I put a set on yer Mama's grave every month or so. Knowing you are out of town and all and I'm over there anyway."

"I wondered who was doing that. That's a real nice thing to do, Cindi. Daddy, the guys and I 'preciate you're thinking of Mama like that."

"I see that you are buying birdseed. Do you have a lot of birds over there? Daddy's yard is just covered with them in the mornings. Probably because he feeds them until they are fat. It's a wonder they can even fly. Squirrels and rabbits, too."

"Yeah, the birds are really startin' to come around my place too. I love to watch them and put out seed for them. They are so pretty."

Glancing at my watch, I noticed that Daddy's strict stomach clock would be going off before I was ready to feed him if I did not hurry. "Sorry to have to rush off, but if Daddy's supper isn't ready on time he will be in a tizzy. Nice seeing you, Cindi."

"Good seein' you, Dana."

Moving rapidly down the aisle, I picked up the last two items I needed from the dairy case. As I turned the corner to the checkout lane, I felt a pull in my chest. Startled, I stopped and without thought ran to find Cindi slowly pushing her cart as if it contained a thousand pounds of birdseed instead of one small bag.

I called over the flashlight display separating us, "Hey, Cindi, how about me and you meeting at the Waffle House for breakfast before I leave this time?" The words came out as if they were self-propelled.

Checking to see if she had heard right, Cindi once again

dab smiled. That hawklike look vanished just for an instant.

"Maybe we can talk about our kids and catch up with each other. You know, have a few laughs about our old school days."

We agreed to meet at 8:00 A.M. the following day. I would fix Daddy's breakfast and have the kitchen cleaned by 7:00. He was still a farmer after all, even if the only livestock he kept were the blue jays in the yard.

Checking out, I rushed to Daddy's and fixed a great supper of his country favorites, trying to ignore the cholesterol count in lieu of the flavor. While dinner cooked, I started the first of several loads of laundry that I would need to complete before bed. Probably should do all the sheets and blankets too while I was here. Especially if I wanted to have even a small bagful by tomorrow morning.

About the Authors

LISA BARRICK: I have been writing on a nonprofessional basis for nearly fifteen years (mostly short stories, novellas, and various other works in progress). I received my B.A. in English from Lincoln Memorial University in 1994, and currently live in Speedwell, Tennessee. I work at The Abraham Lincoln Library and Museum on the campus of Lincoln Memorial University as an office manager and administrative assistant. "The Freedom Quilt" is my first published work.

DONNA BURTON: As a homeschooling mother of five I am, to say the least, active. In addition to writing short fiction stories and magazine articles and working on two different novels, I work forty hours a month for my husband and assist my dear friend with marketing home-education materials nationwide. I love all of the different aspects of my life that God chooses to use when needed, benefiting myself and my family, and others as well.

JEAN FLORA GLICK: I am a public speaker, newspaper columnist, and award-winning writer from Hope, Indiana. My articles and personality profiles have sold to more than twenty-five publications, both secular and religious. My credits include *Writer's Digest*, *Travel & Leisure*, *Indianapolis Woman*, *American Profile*, *McCall's*, and *War Cry* (the magazine of the Salvation Army). My writing has also won national honors through my affiliation with the National Federation of Press Women. I am author of *Holy Smokes! Inspirational Help to Kick the Habit* (Kregel Publications, 2003), letters of encouragement to my daughter Kim, who had a twenty-four-year smoking habit and wanted to quit. I am married to John Glick and have three children and nine grandchildren.

TINA HELMUTH: I live in Grand Rapids, Minnesota. I'm a housewife and I enjoy writing as a hobby. At the time I submitted my short story to Crossings, I was unpublished, but since then I have published my first novel, *Jordan Crossing*.

JOAN JANZEN: I live in Kindersley, Saskatchewan, Canada, with my husband and two sons. I'm employed at a weekly newspaper as a graphic artist. "Hooked on Heaven" is the first story I've written since my high school English class. Placing in a Crossings fiction contest encouraged me to pursue writing. Since then I have had several articles published in magazines in Canada and the United States, and for the past two years I have been writing a weekly muse column. It is very rewarding being able to use the talent God gave me.

CINDY KANE: I live in Eastern Passage, Nova Scotia, Canada, where I am a homemaker, wife, and mother to two teenagers. Although "Eagles' Wings" is my first short story to appear in print, my poetry has appeared in an anthology published by the Poetry Institute of Canada. My hobbies include writing, reading, and crafts.

BETH A. MAURER: I am a transplant to the state of Ohio. Raised in Virginia, I met my husband, Brian, when I came to Ashland University, and have been in the area ever since. Brian and I have been married for sixteen years, and have four children—Angel, Gabrielle, Michael, and Elijah. The Hispanic flavor of my short story comes from my undergraduate work as a Spanish language major, and also from stories of a mission trip my husband made to Mexico. I am a 2004 graduate of Ashland Theological Seminary with a Master of Arts in Clinical Pastoral Counseling, and plan to work with at-risk children and families. My family and I are currently involved with a brand-new church in Ashland, Five Stones Community Church, where I plays keyboard for the worship team.

KAREN MILASINCIC: I live just outside of Butler, Pennsylvania, the small town where my husband and I grew up, and where we also raised our two children. Being a stay-at-home mom was the priority, although I've worked limited hours within some of our family businesses, and most recently as our church's receptionist. I stumbled upon my love of writing after encouragement from a college professor during a brief stab at higher education. Since that single semester more than ten years ago, I've added writing to my other favorite pastimes: quilting, playing the flute, and camping. My contribution to *Hooked on Heaven* is my first published work.

N. MILLER PIPER: Countless books, read and cherished year after year, prompted me to finally attempt creating a story of my own, giving birth to "real" characters that I might know and love. I learned of Jesus at the age of thirty-three, and nine years later Crossings provided a fine opportunity to glorify my Lord. Kevin, my soul mate since age fifteen, works as a locomotive engineer for the Burlington Northern Santa Fe Railway. For years he has provided beautifully for our very busy, often crazy lifestyle. My only child, Jodie, and her husband, Jack, have blessed us with two sweet little grandchildren, August and Emily. I live on eleven acres in southeastern Nebraska, surrounded by many beloved animal friends. I am currently at work on a Christian children's novel, bringing to life and immortalizing some of my dearest animal friends.

VIRGINIA ROARK: I live in Jackson, Missouri, with my husband and four cats. We have two grown children, Chris and Caitlin. After working as a reporter and teaching journalism and writing in college, I'm finally fulfilling my lifelong dream of being of freelance writer. This is my first piece of fiction to be published. I had one short article published in *Discipleship Journal* a couple of years ago.

JAMES SHUMAKER: I live in Newark, Ohio, with my wife and three daughters. On Sundays, I attend Vineyard Grace Fellowship, also in Newark. I am currently a Senior Network Analyst for an international insurance company. Besides serving God, my second biggest passion in life is historical research. Although this is the first time my work has been commercially published, I have written two booklets on my family history, which were distributed among relatives.

CARRIE TURANSKY: I am a native of Oregon and now live in New Jersey. I majored in art at Oregon State University and now pour my creative time and talent into writing. I have won and placed in several writing contests and am a member of American Christian Romance Writers. I have been married to my husband, Scott, for twenty-five years and am the mother of five children and one grandson. Touching hearts with God's love and truth is my goal as I write.